THE
Entanglement

BREANNA J.

SIGN UP!

*Are you on our Email list?
Sign up on our website
www.authorbreannaj.com
or text the word:* **BreannaJ to 866-982-4463**

for discounts, prizes contest and more

CHECK OUT OTHER BOOKS BY AUTHOR BREANNA J.

In the Name of Love

In the Name of Love 2

The Cost of Love

No more secrets

Feelings

Pleasurable Desire

www.authorbreannaj.com

Copyright 2021 by Breanna J
All rights reserved. No part of this book may be reproduced in any form without written consent / permission of the author, except by reviewers who may quote passages to be printed in a newspaper or magazine.

Publisher's Note
This is a work of fiction. Any references, names, characters, businesses, organizations, places, events and incidents are the product of the author's imagination or are used fictionally. any resemblance of actual persons, living or dead, events or locales are entirely coincidental.

Library of Congress Control Number:
ISBN 13: 978-0-578-99199-3

Address: PO Box 24921,
Westgate New York 14624,
United States

Email:info@authorbreannaj.com
Publisher: Epic Dynasty Publishing
Book Cover Designed by Patrick Sparks

LETTER TO MY READERS:

What up Boo,

As always I do hope and pray that this letter finds you well. I am so happy that my faithful readers have been rocking with me since 2018. We have been thru six book releases, tons of short stories, up, down and more. You guys are like my family now. For the ones just joining this ride with me. Welcome to the gang; I hope you are ready for this roll coaster ride I take my readers on with each book.

I appreciate you all in a way you probably will never know or understand, because without every single one of you, I wouldn't be the author I am today.

This book The Entanglement was birth from my short stories of Amber, Dave and Rico that you guys fell in love with. This book took me on an emotional roller coaster ride that made me love and hate each character. I am so hoping that you guys can enjoy every bit of this book, the way I've enjoyed writing it.

Love
Author Breanna J

Check me out in these places

Author Breanna J
www.authorbreannaj.com
www.facebook.com/AuthorBreannaj/
Instagram: Author_Breannaj
www.twitter.com/authorbreannaj
https://www.wattpad.com/user/AuthorBreannaJ

DEDICATION

This book is dedicated to Ravond L Simms a.k.a "My Toot" having you kidnapped while I was writing this book played such a big impact on my mental. I love you nephew forever and always.

This book was also dedicated to Demetris Jackson, my dear friend. I wasn't ready to say bye to you on 9/10/2021 when you took your last breath. I still remember your feedback after reading my first book and now you will never read another. But I promise to do what you told me and never put my pen down.

#TheEntanglement
#AuthorBreannaj

PROLOGUE

Jayden

"YOU READY?" I asked Brandy as I pulled down my ski mask. "Yup let's do this shit cause I got other shit to do." She said to me, "Like what? going out with your friends doing hoodrat shit and screaming hot girl summer?" I asked with a slight laugh as she put her ski mask on, but didn't cover her face just yet. She looked over at me as if I had said the dumbest shit in the world. "Um No! The fuck do I look like? I'm not that type of girl. Just because I live in the hood doesn't mean I do hood bitch shit. I'm trying to get out the hood so I spend my free time in the house studying. Which I could be doing right now instead of doing this illegal shit." She told me. "Then why are you here?" I asked her curiously. "If I told Chase no, he wouldn't have cut my check for school," she said to me with this look on her face.

I knew it was the wrong time, but I was turned on a little by this sexy dark skin woman I had sitting in my car. I looked over at her as she placed her gloves on. There was something about her beauty that was pulling on me. I mean, who wouldn't be turned on by a pretty dark skin bitch that was smart, determined, but also willing to be a rider to the fullest. I licked my lips and then quickly pulled my shit together.

I reached into the back seat and grabbed the black duffle bag I had sitting back there on the floor, and placed it on my lap. I pulled out the two .40-caliber Glocks I had got off of one of my connects. "Can you handle this?" I asked. Brandy looked over at what I had in my hand and sucked her teeth. "Boy, I can handle more than you think I can. The question is, are these shits straight? I don't need shit coming back to me." she said, putting her hand out to get the gun. I handed the gun to her, and as she grabbed it, I looked her in the eyes as I still held the other end of the weapon. "You sure you are ready and you can do this? I can..." before I could finish my sentence, she snatched the gun out of my hand. "Yes! Now let's go." she said and then pulled her ski mask down and then opened the car door. I had to admit I kept questioning Brandy because I wasn't sure about this shit, my damn self. In all the years I was in the game, I never had to do no shit like this. I got out of the game to avoid doing shit that might put the police on my ass, but here I was. I checked my gun and hopped out of the car behind Brandy.

We hurried through the darkness of the night, and I looked around, watching our backs as she led. We got to the front door of our destination, and Brandy stood on the left, and I stood on the right with our guns in our hands, ready. "Knock, " I whispered to her. "Nigga what?" she said, and I could tell from her eyes her face was frowned up under her mask. "Knock," I repeated to her. Brandy put her left hand on her hip as her right one still held on to her gun. "Boy, it's three in the damn morning. This house is pitch black. Ain't nobody answering this damn door. What the fuck do you mean knock." She said to me, "Then how else are we going to get in?" I asked her.

Brandy rolled her eyes and sucked her teeth. "And you

asked if I was ready... Hold this," she said, giving me her gun. Then she squatted down, took a card out of her back pocket and a pin from her hair. I was so busy looking at her firm ass that I didn't even realize how quickly she popped the lock until she stood back up and looked at me. I looked at her, shocked that she even knew how to do some shit like that. "Boy, fix your face. This is still the hood. These white landlords are not putting good locks on these places; they don't think black people are worth it." she whispered and then took her gun back from me.

We walked through the clean house, and I had to admit the inside of the house was way nicer than the outside. We found the stairs and headed up them. We crept up the stairs quickly, and every so often, I took a glance at Brandy's ass to take some tension from the situation. When we got to the top of the stairs, we noticed two rooms with kids sleeping in them. In my head, I was tripping. I had kids of my own, and I didn't want to risk them getting hurt. I straightened up, and we headed down the hall, not making a sound.

We took a few more steps and were at the door of a room where the door was closed. Brandy turned the doorknob and pushed the door open slowly, and I could see two figures in the bed. The room was dark, and nothing but the streetlights coming in from the window gave the room some light. As we moved through the room, we stepped over a bra, a pair of panties, boxers, and condom wrappers on the floor that caught my attention. We stood over the bed with our guns pointed. And I couldn't believe what I was about to do. Brandy gave me a look to go ahead, but I didn't move. That angel was sitting on my shoulder, battling with me about putting a gun to the head of a childhood friend.

I could see Brandy staring at me out of the corner of my eye, but I just couldn't move. She pushed past me, and I felt like

I was watching a movie as everything happened before my eyes. "Wakie wakie nigga." Brandy said before sending the butt of her gun right into Rico's manhood. He jumped out of his sleep, grabbing his meat and his girl that was lying in bed with him jumped up to check on him.

"What the hell are y'all doing here?" she asked after turning on the lamp that was on the nightstand and realizing we were there. She pulled the covers up to shield her naked body. "Bitch, shut up. This has nothing to do with you." Brandy said. "What the fuck is going on?" Rico said in a painful voice, still holding himself. "You don't know, pretty boy?" Brandy asked. "Yo bitch I don't know who you are but clearly you don't know who the fuck I am and you got shit fucked up but I will...."

Brandy cocked her gun and turned her head to the side. "Nigga, you will what?" she said with this voice that made me wonder when this sexy ass woman became a thug. "Rico, baby, who are these people? And why are they in our house? Please, our children are in the next room. Whatever this is about, don't harm them." Rico's baby momma cried out. "Bitch shut up, ain't nobody going to do nothing to your kids as long as ya nigga do right." Brandy said as I noticed Rico reaching under the mattress. I cocked my gun. "Nigga, we just here to deliver a message. Don't make this shit turn into a homicide." I said. "Yeah, please don't..." Brandy agreed.

Rico put his hands up. And for five seconds, I didn't see Rico, the man that had done some fucked up shit, including turning his back on me. I saw Rico, the kid. Rico, that once was my brother. Rico would do anything for me, and I'd do anything for him. "What's the fucking message." Rico said, clearly pissed, but bringing me back to reality.

"We know you snitched to get out." Brandy said Rico's head dropped. "Rico, what are they talking about?" his baby momma asked, looking at him. "Baby, they are lying." Rico said in defense. "Oh, so baby daddy here ain't tell you how his bid got cut down? Okay, well, let me tell you what we aren't lying about; because of your man here, Chase got picked up and is now facing time for a murder charge. A murder that only him, Rico and the deceased person knew about. Now it's funny how suddenly, the feds got a written statement and someone will testify on Chase. And it just so happens all this happens at the same time your man walks out of jail early." the girl's eyes got big. "Rico," she said in disbelief. "I did this for us. You needed me out here. Momma needed me out here." Rico said in a whisper. "So let me explain what him doing that shit for y'all means since he just admitted he did it. That means Chase is missing out on money and you have officially fucked up his life and he's not too happy about that shit. But he's an understanding man, and he knows you have kids to live for. So instead of giving you the stitches that snitches get, you're going to pay up." Brandy said.

"Pay what?" Rico asked with his eyebrow-raising. "Your first payment is for $50,000 and you need to give it to us in 72 hours." Brandy said. "And if I don't," Rico said, turning and looking at me. I felt like he could see through the ski mask and knew it was me. "Well, if you don't, then we are coming back and we'll just kill you. But before we do that, we will kill your girl, your kids, ya baby mom and son you got across town, and the baby momma and daughter you got in Ohio and we won't forget to get your mom too. But we might be doing her a favor, though. She is already dying from stage 4 breast cancer, right?" Brandy said.

I looked over at her. I was shocked at how she was holding this shit down. Chase told me she had been through some shit in her past that made her tough and a rider, but he didn't tell me she was like this. Hell, she didn't even need me. She was harder than a few niggas I had come across.

Rico's jaw tightened "and where the fuck am, I supposed to get $50,000 in 72 hours." he asked. "That is not for me to figure out. That sounds like a you problem you might want to handle before everyone you love pays for your fuck up," Brandy said. "I can't get $50,000 in 72 hours," Rico said. "What did I just say? Or I can just start taking people out now, so you see how serious we are." Brandy said, pointing her gun at Rico's girl. "No, no, no, he will get the money." She cried out as tears rolling down her face. "Where the fuck am I supposed to get that money?" Rico said, as he turned and looked at her. "Better go ask that little light skin girl that you be in and out of those fancy-ass hotels with. I'm sure she got money cause there's no way you're living in this neighborhood but paying for them hotels' ' Brandy said, and I looked at her with my eyes wide. "Light skin girl... hotels." Rico's baby momma shouted with fear leaving her voice and the black ghetto girl taking over. Brandy laughed in an evil voice. "Seems like y'all got some shit to figure out we are going to get out of here, but here, take this in 72 hours. You will get a call on that number telling you where to drop the money. Don't miss it and don't fuck up. I'd hate to have to come back," Brandy said, throwing Rico a little flip phone. "And once I get y'all this $50,000, am I set and clear," Rico asked. "You'll be set and clear when Chase says you are. Good night," Brandy said as she turned to the door and walked out.

I followed behind her, still facing Rico and his girl with my gun still pointed at them to avoid anything going wrong. "This is some bullshit," Rico said as he reached under the bed. "Move" I yelled at Brandy, thinking shit was about to go left. But to my surprise, she turned and busted her gun. Rico and his girl ducked. And without finding out if Brandy's bullets hit anyone, we ran down the stairs and out of the house as the sound of the gunshots and screaming faded. We got outside and hauled ass back to my car. We jumped in, and I sped off down the street as we ripped our ski mask off. Brandy was smiling from ear to ear. But we were both panting.

"You think he's going to pay up?" I asked her. "Chase is your brother. Have you ever known a mutha fucker not to pay him what they owe him?" I was silent because she had a point. Chase was not a mutha fucker to be played within or out of jail. This nigga could make shit happen that even I wouldn't believe had I not witness most of it for myself. The last time he got picked up, he spent three months in jail. He made more money while he was in prison than he made in one month while he was free. But Chase never failed to amaze me. He was just that nigga, and his name alone spoke volumes. Everyone knew who he was. And with a girl like Brandy in his corner, how couldn't he.

"question, what was up with you upping the price though. Chase said hit that nigga for $25,000 not $50,000." I said to her, "shit we got to see this shit through for him, so we should walk away with something too. You had to admire the hustler in this girl. I'm not sure about you, but $12,500 would come in handy for me, especially with Chase being where he is right now. I got school to worry about, and my own personal stuff. So if I'm putting my ass on the line, it ain't going to be for free. Not even for a nigga that's giving me dick," she said.

I looked over at Brandy, and she was taking all the extra stuff off. "How did you know all that info about Rico?" I asked her. "I do my research." She answered. I got to a red light and stopped. I looked around to make sure we weren't being followed. Then I looked at Brandy. "You've been looking at me like that all night, what's up?" she asked me. "I'm just shocked," I told her, "About?" She said back, "You're just so fine. From your physical appearance to the way you just handled that situation. I would have never expected that from you with all the other times I've seen you in the past," I said. "Really?" she said in a shy way. "Yes," I told her.

Brandy looked down at her hands and then back at me. It's crazy how she was just Billy badass; now she was playing shy. "When we get to my place, you should come in. That way we can plan what's next." She said to me, I sat there for a moment, thinking, before I finally said, "Nah, Imma let you go study and get up with you later. I got to get rid of all this shit from tonight." I told her. Brandy nodded her head for a moment and then grabbed my face and pulled me in, and pressed her soft lips against mine as her tongue entered my mouth and entangled with mine. I put my hand on her back and pushed her as close to me as I could with the armrest being between us. The feeling of her breast pressing against her hand resting on my face felt so welcoming. When we released each other, she looked me in the eye. "Come inside so we can plan what's next..." she said in a seductive voice.

Amber

THE RAYS of the sun came peering into our bedroom windows, awaking me just like they did every morning. I opened my eyes and looked around the room. Every day it still amazed me the lifestyle I was able to live. The girl from the ghetto that left her momma's house at a young age and almost didn't graduate, the girl that most people counted out, now lived in a three-bedroom house in a gated community with a BMW outside to drive. And a lawyer boyfriend who made six figures, and he hadn't even made a partner yet. But what do you expect from one of the best criminal lawyers out there? Talk about leveling up. I had done alright for myself, and it was all thanks to Dave.

I rolled over and faced the handsome man I had been sharing a bed with for years now. His caramel skin was glowing in the sunlight, or maybe it was the diamond earrings he had in his ears. I stared at this man and admired him for a while as I rubbed my finger through his beard and watched the light as it hit my 2.08 Carat Princess Lab Diamond engagement ring.

Dave rolled over in the bed with his eyes still closed, kissed my chest, and rubbed his hand on my thighs. All these years together, and our morning routine was almost always the same. Either he had an important meeting, was up and on the go, or was trying to get it in before he went to work. From His action, I knew what it was going to be today.

"Good Morning Beautiful," he finally said to me in between, giving my breast more kisses. "Good morning handsome." I said back to him, smiling. His eyes opened, and he looked up at me, showing me his light brown eyes and a damn near perfect smile. As he rubbed on my thighs more, I rubbed my hand across his beard and stared at him until Dave lifted his head, hinting for me to kiss him. I closed my eyes, taking in this perfect moment. Dave then sat up in bed and moved his kisses from my lips to my neck. He knew exactly where my spot was. And every time he hit it, I couldn't stop myself from getting turned on.

Dave pulled the cover back and eased my legs apart. Without moving his head from my spot on my neck, he lifted his body and got between my legs, and I laid back in the bed. As he hovered over me, I relaxed and looked him in the eyes. "Damn, you're beautiful," he said to me. It was something I had heard all my life, but it still made me blush. Maybe it was because I don't think of myself as beautiful. Sexy, yes. But beautiful no. I don't know why most people would think they were the same. But I believed sex appeal was something you could learn. Beauty was something you just had or didn't have. Beauty was way more than skin deep.

Dave raised my nightgown, and I lifted my body from the bed, helping him get it up. He kissed every inch of my body before cupping my b cup breast in his hands and then sucking on my nipples. I moaned out in pleasure. Dave left my breast and made his way down my stomach and then to my pelvis and from there to my pussy. I watched him as he worked because it made me even more turned on.

But when Dave got to my pussy and ate, the excitement I had built up quickly left. Dave licked my pussy like a cat licking milk, and I hated the fact that instead of sucking on my clit, he would pull on it and my pussy lips. And that was all before he took his finger and exposed my clit. I was trying so hard to focus on something else, visioning porn in my mind so that this morning wouldn't be like other mornings and I could actually get my nut. But before I knew it, Dave was done licking, and he was sliding his dick in me, not even realizing that I was not at the same point he was at. I laid there moaning and faking every bit of pleasure, just waiting for the three minutes and 55 seconds to be over. All these years, this man still didn't know how to satisfy my body, but he swore every time we had sex that he was beating the pussy up.

In three minutes, just like I expected, I felt Dave's dick jump. Then he went into overdrive, pounding on my pussy until he finally burst. And I followed along, pretending like I had come with him when I knew as soon as he went to take a shower I could pull out my lipstick vibrator from Bedroom Kandi and get myself right.

Dave laid next to me in bed, breathing hard as I looked at the ceiling. "Damn girl, that pussy is always so good." he said to me. I smiled. "Just for you, baby," I told him. "What did I do to get so lucky?" he said and then kissed my cheek. "I'm the lucky one baby." I told him in a cute little voice. "Let's just say we are lucky together. And hopefully that luck will show up at work today." Dave said as he sat on the edge of the bed. "Hard case at work today?" I asked him. "Nah, not today baby, I still have the same case I've been working on, but if things go the way I want it to, our lives could change forever. Today if that board calls my name doing the meeting I will be a partner. That means more money, less work, that means we officially hit the next level." Dave said. "Well bae, it will happen. You've worked hard for this moment." I told him as I crawled across the bed and rubbed his back.

Dave grabbed my left hand and brought it up to his mouth, and kissed it. "Thank you for always being so supportive and being my rock bae," he said to me. "I'm just being to you what you are to me." I told him, "Okay, let me get up and get in the shower and get this day started. Before I be back knee deep in that pussy and late to work." Dave said after letting my hand go and letting out a deep breath. I laid back in the middle of the bed, stretched out as I watched his naked body. I know it was an odd thing to admire on a man, but I always thought he had a nice butt, and the tattoo that said I am their keeper on his back was nice, too. "I am their keeper," I said out loud. Dave turned and looked at me. "You are that them. For you and momma, I live, and for you and her, I will die. "I smiled and blew Dave a kiss. I was no fool. I knew Dave had that tattoo before I came along. But he was secretive about certain parts of his past, so I just accepted the way he serenaded me with love.

Dave gathered his stuff for his shower. Before he walked out of the room, he stopped and looked at me. "You're so beautiful," he said, admiring me this time with more amazement in his voice, and then gave me another kiss on the lips and walked out the room.

Once I heard the shower come on and Dave started to sing, I rolled over to my nightstand and grabbed my cell. I opened it up and sent a text. Good morning handsome; you were on my mind this morning. Have a great day. Kisses, I hit send and then put the phone back down. I pulled my vibrator from the nightstand and quickly pleased myself to the thought of my best-kept secret.

And although I knew I was wrong on so many levels and felt so much guilt, I couldn't help it. I had a love for Dave, and I was happy with the lifestyle I had because of him, but the things I needed sexually I wasn't getting from him, and it had driven me into another man's arms. But I knew I had to stop. I planned to go to a meeting today to discuss this with other women in the same boat as me or similar.

It was funny. I never thought there would be women in a help group for something like this. Or that I would even go to one. I had to stop cheating on Dave. Our wedding would be here before I knew it, and I didn't want to be one of those wives. I would have to cope with what I didn't get from him sexually because he gave me everything else I needed.

As I finished up, Dave was getting out of the shower. He came out and got dressed, and I got up, threw on my robe, and headed to the kitchen to make his coffee. By the time I was done and coming out of the kitchen with his lunch in one hand and his coffee mug in the other, Dave was fully dressed and running out of our room. He stopped me at the stairs and kissed me on my cheek. "I feel it bae; today is going to be life changing." He said and then walked away happily. I listened as he walked out the front door, and then I heard him get into his car. I went to the window to watch him drive away and said to myself, "Amber, looks like today is the day you need to decide and get your shit together or you're going to lose it all playing."

RICO

"SO REMARIO, how are you feeling today?" the doctor asked me. "Every day that I'm home and not in some cage is a day that I feel good." I answered him. When in actuality, I was stressed and tired. One bullet grazed me after everything that happened last night, and Toni made me go to the emergency room. We were there for hours, and the entire time, Toni was running her mouth about how I was going to get the money and who the fuck was the bitch I had been with.

It got to be so much that, eventually; I had to tell her to shut the fuck up. I had enough on my plate. The cops were supposed to keep everything confidential, so how the fuck did Chase know I did it. Not to mention the voice of one of the people he sent to my house seemed so familiar. It reminded me of this nigga Jayden. But Jayden had turned a new leaf, and I knew he would do no shit like that. Especially not to me.

"I understand your thoughts on this, but how does your body feel," he asked me. "I mean, seeing that I am slowly dying, it feels pretty damn outstanding," I told him in a sarcastic voice. "Listen, Remario, just because you have H.I.V does not mean you are dying." the doctor said to me. "Listen, doc, you ain't gotta lie to me. I have come to grips that God has a funny sense of humor, and this disease he let me get is just another part of that. I am just lucky I can spend the time I have left with my children and my family." I told him. "And as long as you keep taking your medicine, you will have plenty more days. Give us a few minutes, and I will have a nurse come in here with some papers I want you to look over while you're at home, and then you're free to go," the doctor said.

It was easy for a white doctor to think I would not die because he didn't know me. He didn't know the shit I had done in my past or the story behind how I got this disease. All he knew was that I was here and that medicine could keep me alive. But what I knew was that my days were numbered if this disease didn't kill me, them mutha fuckers Chase sent to my house last night would because I did not know how the fuck I was going to get the $50,000 they wanted, and I was running out of time.

All I knew was I had to protect my family by any means necessary. I had Toni questioning whether she and the kids were safe or needed to go down south with her parents. And the way my phone kept ringing with Bianca and Monique's name let me know that as soon as I dropped Toni and the kids at the house to come to this appointment, she got her ass on the phone and called my other two baby mommas. These bitches didn't even like each other, but they were going to bond the fuck together to stress me the fuck out. Like I wasn't stressed enough, feeling like I couldn't protect them.

It was still hard to understand how I went from riches to rags. Old Rico wouldn't even have to deal with no shit like this. I had it all, and then I watched it all just wash away. I had to admit I was tripping when I got caught up. Dave and Jayden had just told me they were pulling out the game on me, and I was pissed. I was not like them niggas; I didn't have businesses and degrees to fall back on. All I knew was this lifestyle, and it was good to me until it wasn't.

And it was all because my so-called brothers switched up on me. I never thought I could hate the niggas. I got it out of the mud with the niggas I called my brothers the way I do. I mean these were my niggas, we went from diapers to men together. I had starved with these niggas, learned the game with these niggas, and when we got put on, these were the niggas I ate with. We all were all we had. From different mothers, but the same struggle and going through that hunger together made us family. It seems like I remember this shit like it just happened yesterday, how this shit all unfolded.

Dave, Jayden, and I were kicking it like we usually did. We were counting our money and having a few drinks. We were young niggas in the game, but we had been doing this shit with ease for years now. No police, no fuck-ups, no nothing. Even the O.Gs in the hood had respect for us. They called us the three pretty niggas and couldn't understand how we were making this shit seem so easy with no issues. It was pretty simple; we stayed humble and in our lane. We weren't trying to take anyone's territory or step on anyone's toes; that made a lot of niggas have respect for us.

Not to mention Jayden came up with this idea for us all to go to school to learn how to cut hair. Then he used some of his money to open a barbershop, and for all the banks and government knew all of us worked there. Then he opened a laundromat and a soul food restaurant. At the same time, Dave was taking his money and putting himself through law school. I was the only one just making my money and just getting by.

But as well as things were, I couldn't deny that I felt like my brothers were changing on me. "Yo, I need to talk to ya about some real shit." Dave said as we sat at the table, and he took a sip of his drink. "What's on your mind, broty?" I asked him. "I think I might get out of the game soon," Dave said. "Nigga, you sound crazy," I told him. "No lie, I have been thinking the same thing." Jayden said, "what the fuck is wrong with y'all we living our best life right now. We get money, bitches... man life is good, why would Y'all want to change that shit." I said, looking at these niggas like they were crazy.

"Rico man, this shit was never the ultimate plan for my life. I'm trying to be a lawyer. Selling drugs just made that shit a possibility because coming from where we come from, it was either no school or going into debt trying to make a better future for myself. Now I have more than enough money to finish school, so I'm good. I want out before people start to figure out what we really got going on." Dave said to me. "Nigga, why not be a lawyer and still get this bread?" I told him. Dave started laughing. "nigga when have you ever heard of a drug-dealing lawyer." Dave said.

To me, there was nothing wrong with how we were living and for Dave to be a lawyer and keep up what we had going on. At least then, if we got caught up in some shit, we had someone to get us out of it. "Bruh, that's the whole point. No one would ever think a damn lawyer was a drug dealer. It would be the perfect cover." I said. "Ric, I'm not looking for a cover." Dave said. "yo you're really crazy, but I'm with Dave. It's time to get out while we are ahead. No feds are on us, nothing, let's take our luck and move on before it runs out on our asses." Jayden said. "you niggas not thinking what about the family?" I said, "Nigga, that's exactly what I'm thinking about. I got a damn baby on the way that I need to be around to raise. And you already have four kids and three baby mommas Ric. My businesses are doing good and bringing in money. I can give my dope boy lifestyle up to be a business owner and a father." Jayden said. "you niggas are tripping. I'm not getting out the game and neither are y'all because Y'all made a pack that as long as one of us was in this lifestyle we all were. Remember the tattoos that we all have on our backs. I am their keeper. You niggas are supposed to be my keepers and I'm yours. You niggas are supposed to ride for me, no matter what." I said.

"Ric, you can't hold us to something we said when we were young and dumb. We agreed to that shit when we thought we didn't have shit to live for but the money." Dave said. "So we get out of the game and then what about me? What the fuck am I supposed to do? This shit... drugs... this is all I know. This shit keeps a roof over me, momma and my kids' heads; so how am I supposed to survive and provide if I don't sell drugs no more." I said to them, "bro come work at the barbershop with me." Jayden said.

I looked at that nigga like he had just lost his damn mind. "So I'm supposed to go from being a boss to being your employee; what the fuck do I look like," I said. Then what are you interested in? We have to think differently; fast money can't be how we live forever." Dave said, "are you not hearing me, my nigga? This is all I know. This is all I am interested in, and I'm not about to go back to being a little nigga now because you niggas are deciding to switch on me. y'all my brothers, right?" I said, getting loud and angry to the point where I wanted to flip the table over. "You know we are. Your brothers; blood couldn't make us any closer." Jayden said, "then ride with me." I said, "Bro, I can't agree to do this with you for the rest of my life." Dave said. "Yeah, bro, same here. I can't promise you that either.' Jayden said.

"So Y'all telling me that this is it Y'all are going to throw away our friendship and brotherhood." I said. "No one said that dumb shit but you. Us wanting out has nothing to do with the brotherhood. We are brothers no matter what road we all decide to go back to." Jayden said, "it does because Y'all know Chase knows all three of us, not just me. So y'all leaving me is fucking me over." I said. "Man, I ain't know your ass was going to take it like this." Dave said. "Well, I am! yall taking money out of my pocket. This is how I handle my responsibility as a man." I said.

Dave took a deep breath and said, "Listen, I'm out of the game, period. I can't change my mind about that, but because we are family, I will still show up to the meeting and stuff with Chase. But this shit is all about you. You control it all," Dave said. "Cool, no problem. I respect that that's real brother shit. I can handle this shit on my own. Jayden, can you agree to do the same thing, bro? Just show up to the meeting, you don't have to do anything else." I said.

Jayden sat at that table quietly. "So you take that long to decide if you are going to take food out of my kid's mouth or not?" I asked. "Bro, I can't do it. I will not agree with it. Dave and I showing up to those meetings mean we still attached to this lifestyle and if you fuck up, that's all of our asses." Jayden said. "that's fucking crazy, so you have no faith in me. you know I can do this shit on my own?" I asked. "That's not what I am saying because I know your a get money niggas so you going to make sure shit stay a float to the best of your ability but I also know that when it's just one person controlling everything in a business like this, it's easy to fuck up. We have been good for so long because it was three of us and we checked each other. With Dave and me out of the way, there's no one here to do that." Jayden said.

My anger got the best of me, and I grabbed my gun off the table. "Nigga, either you can be a silent partner in this shit and just be a body in the meeting or you can be a dead body no one needs." I said, "Rico, chill man, put that gun down. We brothers, you know, we don't pull out our damn guns on each other. You letting that Remy get the best of you." Dave said Jayden sat at the table looking at me with a death stare. "that's how we giving it up my nigga? I'm your brother and you pull a gun on me because I was trying to help you? Fuck you, Ric," Jayden said to me. "Both yall chill the fuck out," Dave said.

The tension in the room was thick enough to cut with a knife, and I had never felt more alone than I did at that very moment. "Rico, listen, you got to respect how Jay feels." Dave said. "why should I when he doesn't give a fuck about me?" I said, "man I want more from you, that's what a brother is supposed to do." Jayden said, "Fuck you, Jay." I yelled.

"Ric, listen, if Chase doesn't want to fuck with you by yourself, then so be it we can find another connect for you. But don't ruin the brotherhood over this shit." Dave tried to plead. "You'll always be my brother cause you always looked out and we are blood family, but fuck Jay, we ain't shit no more, ain't no brothers when it comes to me and him." I said. "Shit says no more than nigga get the fuck out my shit then this mutha fucking building in my name nigga." Jayden said, "no problem nigga say less. Let's divide the money. All of it too! Including the money in the safes and on this table and I'm all the way good." I said, that night I walked away from that table a wealthy nigga but brother less in my head.

"Mr. Peris," the nurse said as she opened the door and took me from my thoughts. "Yeah," I said, looking at her. "Here's the papers the doctor wanted you to have. One of those papers has information for the therapist and another a help group that has people in the same situation as you." She said to me, "Little momma, I got H.I.V. There is nothing a therapist or help group can do for me." I told her. "Damn," she said, looking me up and down. "Oh, my god I am so sorry." She told me. "It's all good love, no hard feeling that was my exact reaction when I found out." I told her. "I'm just saying you are way too fine to have those types of issues." She said, "Yup, now my fine ass is deadly in more ways than one. Am I free to go?" I asked her as a text came through on my phone and took my attention. I got up, took the papers from her, and headed to the door.

Amber

BEFORE GOING INTO THE BATHROOM, I went to my bedroom window and watched Dave leave. Something about when he wasn't around brought me so much freedom compared to how I had to be when he was around. I began my typical day-to-day routine. "Alexa play Broke by Ari Lennox," I said as I started to dance to the beat as it dropped and then headed to the bathroom.

    I turned the shower on and then went to the sink to put on my face mask as the water heated up. Once the water was perfect, I jumped in. I made sure my body was smooth as a baby's bottom, and there was no hair anywhere. I made it my business always to step correctly, so that I was representing Dave in the best way at all times. I was anal about making sure nothing was ever out of place. Everything had to be perfect at all times, from my wigs and sew-ins down to my toenail polish; that way, I always fit in Dave's world. Dave and I had been together in all the time; he had never seen me looking rough. To him, I was like a barbie doll; I was perfect at all times. I didn't even take my hair out around him. He was the definition of black excellence, so I had to be perfect.

Even the house we lived in was perfect. It was a townhouse in a gated community. It was white on the outside, and once a year, Dave had it pressure washed to keep the white color. A white fence surrounded it, and it looked just like every other house on our street. Everything inside the house was all white, and I spent most of my time cleaning, so there was never dirt anywhere. After seeing how some of the partners at Dave's firm lived, I always wanted our house to match up to that.

I took pride in my body, so I was always in and out of the spa and the gym. And I was always buying a new waist trainer from Soso snatched. Or doing whatever to keep me right and tight. I even made cleaning work out. I got out of the shower and checked myself out in the mirror that hung on the back of the bathroom door. As I spun around to check out my ass, I saw my one imperfection I could not get rid of. It was a burn that was on my lower back. Most people thought it was just a birthmark. But because I spent so much time putting cocoa butter and shea butter on it to control what it looked like. But it was the reminder of what I left behind. It was a reminder of how perfection can be so damaged and broken. It reminded me of how my mom treated me and why I had a hard time believing in love. The one person who was supposed to love me the most. Hate me and hurt me to the point I didn't care when she died to say my last goodbyes.

I spun back around and smiled at myself. "Damn I'm getting thick." I thought out loud because I was gaining weight in all the right places. I exited the bathroom and went back to our bedroom. I picked up my phone off the nightstand and laid across the bed, and took a picture of my body. Once I got the right picture, I rolled over on my stomach to send a text. "What man doesn't like nudes during the day," I said.

I sent the picture off and then began to lotion my body. Some time had gone by, and there was no response from Dave, and I figured he had made it to work and was busy. So I sent another text. This time I got an answer instantly. Damn girl, you are looking good. That pussy looks like it needs to feel this dick. Get us a room at the Hyatt we always go to, and I will be there in an hour.

A bright smile came over me. And although Dave and I had just had sex not too long ago, I wasn't thinking or caring about that unfulfilling situation because I knew this round was going to be everything I wanted and more. I opened my hotels.com app and booked a room at the Hyatt for immediate check-in. Because of how many times we went there, they gave me a discount. I had a prepaid card. I normally stashed the money I took from Dave. I used that to pay for the room, and then I called the hotel and requested an immediate check-in.

Then I wasted no time getting ready. I went into the bathroom and removed my face mask and brushed my teeth. I put my hair up in a messy bun and threw on my contacts to hide my eye. My sister Brandy and Dave were the only people that knew I had two different colored eyes. I thought it was weird and made me feel like something that should be in one of those x-man movies. But Dave thought it was beautiful and unique. He asked me to stop wearing my contacts. But this was my comfort. Not to mention the one hazel eye and the one dark brown eye was the one thing my mom always reminded me I got from my daddy. And since he didn't have the nerve to stick around and be a part of my life. I had no desire to look anything like him.

Once I was done in the bathroom, I went back into our room and found some black leggings and a black Chanel shirt to put on. I paired it with my black Chanel sandals, sunglasses, purse, and, of course, my Chanel number 5 perfume. Once I was dressed, I grabbed one of my oversized purses from the closet and threw a change of clothes in there.

When I had everything I needed, I headed out of the house and to my car. I got into the car, and before I pulled off, I checked a few things. First, I made sure that none of my nosey White neighbors were watching me. Then I took the condoms from my glove box and placed them in my bag and finally turned off my location on my iPhone. Just in case Dave checked my location, I didn't want him to see me at the hotel. Once I was good, and I applied some lip gloss, and I pulled off.

It took me no time to get to the hotel. I got the room key and went up to our room. I sent a text letting him know the room number. Then I checked out the room before getting comfortable, making sure everything was nice and clean. Then I undress down to just my black bra and panties. And waited for the knock at the door.

When I finally heard it, I almost broke my neck, being thirsty and running to the door. I peeked through the door hole, and as soon as I saw Rico, I swung the door open. "Damn you looking good." He said to me as he stepped in, and I stepped back, showing him what I was working with; with a massive smile on my face. "Thank you, baby." I said to him,

There was no reason to beat around the bush; I was already hot and ready, like a little caesar's pizza. Rico closed the door, and I was on him with no hesitation. "So what lie did your tell you nigga this time to be here with me?" Rico asked with a laugh. It was something about the comfort I had with Rico, so I didn't hide from him. I had a man. He was very aware that I was unhappy sexually, and outside of that, he wanted to know nothing else. Not even Dave's name.

I put my finger to Rico's lips as I looked him in the eyes. "We are not talking about him." I said in a sexy voice, before biting my lip as I unbuckled his pants. I dropped down to my knees and pulled Rico's dick out, and was face to face with it. It was always the niggas that you weren't supposed to have that gave you the best dick. Rico had length and width. I was really about to let his dick hit that little thing in the back of my throat. But he stopped me.

"fuck all that. I am ready to dive in." He said as he bent down and scooped me up. "But I want to suck the soul from your dick. My mouth is watering for it." I said as he slowly carried me to the bed with his pants down to his ankles. "Maybe another time," he answered quickly as he laid me down on the bed. I had to admit it was odd that Rico never wanted me to give him head. Mainly because I was great at it; all I wanted was that one moment to look up and see his eyes roll in the back of his head and know that I did that to him.

Rico pushed my panties to the side and licked his lips at the sight of my pussy. He began to gently rub on her. And I spread my legs, giving him all the room he needed. Rico massaged my pussy and until my lips spread for him. He applied a little pressure as he rubbed on my clit, but not enough to make me feel like he was a DJ and I was his mixing board. I let out a slight moan. "you like that." He asked. "Yes baby. Now hurry and get inside me. I want to feel you." I said. "Do you really?" he asked and then took his middle finger and slid in me. He fingerstroked me a few times before he finally said. "Yeah, you're ready." I sat up, and Rico placed his hand to my face, and I took every finger and licked it down as I enjoyed the taste of my own juices.

.Rico pulled a condom from his pants pocket, and I removed my panties as he slid it on. Once Rico was strapped, it was go time. He entered me, and my lady box rejoiced. With every stroke, I tightened my pussy muscles to make sure I didn't cum too quickly. "Take that bra off. I want to see them titties bounce," Rico commanded. In between moans and trying to contain myself, I eased my top half up and removed my bra without stopping what was happening to my lower.

Rico put his head down and took one of my titties into his mouth. He sucked on it and massaged my nipples with his tongue in a way that made me get wetter. I let out a moan, and Rico didn't stop; he moved over to the other side and repeated what he had done. I place my hand on his head as if he was a baby nurse. That was, until Rico came up for air.

He placed his hand around my neck, and I bit on my bottom lip in excitement. Rico pounded on my pussy, and although it was enjoyable, it wasn't his norm. I looked at him, and he seemed zoned out. "Oh my god baby," I moaned out, and Rico took his hand from around my neck and placed it in my mouth. When he removed his hands from my lips, he grabbed my legs and held them up in the air as he beat my pussy up. I held on to the hotel sheets with my eyes closed, knowing I was reaching my climax. "yes baby, right there," I said to Rico. "You like that shit? Cum on this dick then." He said to me, "Go deeper," I instructed. Rico let go of my legs and separated them wide. And sent every inch of his manhood into me, and I gasped for air as I reached out for him.

Rico pushed my hands away from that I had on his chest. "Nah, don't push me away now. You said deeper." He said to me, "But I am about to cum baby." I said a moan. "Good," Rico said as he licked his index finger and rubbed my clit with it. And I lost the battle I was trying to hold on to and came all over his dick.

"Turn over," Rico demanded. I rolled over on all fours and put my arch in my back. Rico placed one of his feet on the bed on my side and guided his dick back inside of me. "Hell yeah," he moaned out. "fuck" I moan, trying not to bury my face in the covers. Rico eased one of his fingers into my ass, and I knew it was only going to be a matter of time before I was coming all over his dick again.

I looked back at him and threw this ass back. Biting down

on my lip as I watched and enjoyed the sounds of our bodies connecting together. Rico wrapped his hand back around my neck and this time pulled me closer to him. And I felt him better this way than the missionary position, that niggas was in my guts while hitting it from the back like this. He went into overdrive, and I did everything I could to make sure that my legs didn't give out under me as I came again.

But Rico didn't stop. "Bae, oh my god you have to stop. I feel like I have to pee." I yelled out. "Nah, I've finally got you to that point. Don't run from it. go ahead and squirt for me." He said from behind me. "But..." and before I could finish my sentence, a sensation I had never felt before took over my body as I released it. and my body gave out cause me to lay flat on the bed on my stomach.

Rico pulled out and sat on the edge of the bed. As I gathered myself and tried to catch my breath I looked at the condom and realized he didn't nut. "Are you okay?" I asked as I sat up on the edge of the bed next to him. "Yeah, I'm good. Why do you ask that" He answered back. Quickly. "because it's not like you not to cum. I said, drawing attention to the empty condom. "I just got some shit on my mind, and I needed to let off some of the shit I had built up, but as long as you got what you needed, we all good." He said to me, "Talk to me," I said to him, getting closer. "Nothing to talk about ain't shit you can do to change what I got going on." He said to me, "Well damn, just make me feel like nothing." I said to him, "Nah, it's not even like that for real. It's just that I am honest with myself. The time that we share is more than good enough; just know that." He said to me,

We sat there in silence, and all I wanted was for Rico to let down that wall and let me in. Rico's phone rang, and he pulled it out of his pocket. He looked at the flip phone and then at me. He got up quickly and went to the bathroom. I sat quietly trying to hear what he was saying in there, but I heard nothing outside of I ain't got it yet. Startly after that, the toilet flushed. And Rico came out fully dressed. "Yo I got to go." He said to me,

"No round two?" I asked him as I got up and walked over to him and wrapped my arms around his neck. "As much as I want to, I can't today." He said to me and then slapped me on the ass. "I love you," I told him. Rico looked at me with his eyebrows raised. 'You don't have to say it back. I just need you to know how I feel. I am always here for you, and I will do anything for you." I said to him,

"Aight shawty Imma hit you later. You be safe." He said to me as He unwrapped my arms from around his neck and headed to the door. I stood there in shock because although I knew the situation we had was crazy, I never expected it to go like that.

I sat on the bed in deep thought as my phone rang. I went over to my purse and pulled out my phone to see Dave's mother's number. I rolled my eyes at the thought of having to deal with her. And let the phone ring until it went to voicemail. In a matter of minutes, she texted me. Well, since your screening my call, I hope you're going to be at this wedding dress fitting about on time.

Lord knows I did not know why Ms. Dorthie hated me the way she did. I did everything to try and gain her approval. But it was a losing battle, so I did what I could to smile around her and bite my tongue because of the way her son loved her. But deep down inside, I wanted her ass to get cancer again and die from it this time.

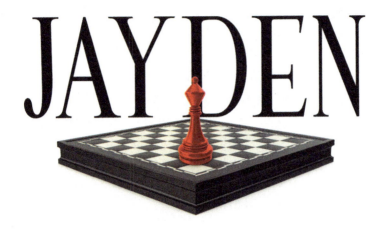

JAYDEN

THE SOUND of my phone ringing pulled me out of my sleep as the rays of the sun hit my eyes. I sat up on the couch and looked around my office as I rubbed my eyes. "Shit Tracy's going to kill me." I said to myself when I realized I had fallen asleep at the barbershop and never took my ass home. I had only stopped by here to get rid of the evidence from last night. I was going to throw everything in the furnace and go on about my night.

Brandy's ass had me horny as a bitch after seeing her in action. She was about five-five with a milk chocolate skin tone, these dark green eyes that sucked you in, and a body other bitches dreamed of. Thick lips, nice breasts, wide hips, and a nice fat ass. But I resisted. I declined her offer to come up to her place and all. I figured I'd make this quick move and then go home and fuck the shit out of my baby momma Tracy's ass. I mean, if nothing else, street life taught me you should finish handling business before you lay with any bitch, and you sure don't mix business and pleasure. Fucking Brandy ass would get me caught up on so many levels.

I stood up and stretched; my phone rang again, and I

glanced at it. I EXPECTED TO SEE TRACY CALLING when I picked it up from between the couch cushions, but it wasn't her. It was a call from Attica. I looked at the clock, and it was 9:30 am. I answered the phone quickly.

"Hello," I answered

"You have a collect call from... Chase," the recording said. Before the machine could go through the long message to follow, I pressed one for the call to start.

"Yo, what's good, big bro?" I said into the phone. "Was that package delivered?" Chase asked in his deep voice, getting straight to the point. "Yeah, it was," I told him. "Good, good..." he said. "Why you ain't tell me the bitch Brandy was so raw?" I asked. "Yeah, Shawty is badder than a mutha fucker. And that little bitch is always down for whatever. Not to mention the pussy is good and the head even better. And she can fight from what I heard. Nights in here, I think about her ass more than I think about wifey." He said to me, "You better not let your crazy ass wife hear you saying that shit." I told him with a laugh. "Man, she already knows how I am. But never get it twisted; the bitch Brandy is down for whatever because she is trying to survive. I met her when she was going through some shit, and then her momma died. She had nothing but a bunch of anger towards the world. I helped her get on her feet, and she has been down to ride for me ever since. But as smart as she is, the bitch is a little dumb." He said.

That bitch seemed more intelligent than a muthafucker to me last night." I said, "I say that because she is so stuck on surviving that she is gullible and easy to manipulate. "How do you figure that, bro?" I asked. "Nigga, I'm in jail and I'm still controlling the bitch and know for sure that she ain't giving the pussy away or anything else." he said, laughing.

"You one lucky ass nigga." I told him as I joined in the laugh. "Nah, I'm not lucky I'm needed. That bitch needs me to make her life continue. She has no one but me. But I am careful with her. That bitch plays nice with her sister and really hates her. She talked to me about it on more than one occasion, so if a bitch will play with their family I will be careful about how they treat me." he said to me.

"Her sister? Amber?" I asked. "Yup, that bitch hates her." he told me. Now that was a surprise to me. When I met up with Brandy last night, that wasn't the first time we had been around each other. She got a big sister named Amber, that thick almond colored shorty that my bro Dave wifed up. I had been to their house occasionally, and Brandy was there. But Brandy never showed a bit of hate for or towards Amber. It was always so much love, it seemed like. I figured they were close as hell since they lost their mom.

A lot of noise started in Chase's background, and he said to me, "Nigga, these dummies in here trying to fight let me hang the fuck up before these crackers get to acting stupid. But yo little bro, you need to come up here and check me asap. I love you kid." he said before the line went dead. From the sound of Chase's voice, I knew he was expecting me up there today or sometime this week to discuss something he couldn't say over the phone. As grown as I was, Chase still made sure I knew he was the big brother and I would do what he said. Sometimes that shit fucked with my pride. But he was the only bloodline I had, so I sucked it up.

I sat back on the couch and closed my eyes. I couldn't believe that I really did that shit last night. I got it out of the mud with Rico. He was my brother once upon a time. I was there when he and Toni gave birth to their first child, and last night I was in their home holding them at gunpoint. This was some crazy shit. Even though Rico had pulled a gun on me once before, I never thought I'd do the shit back to him. And I couldn't even respect myself for how I did it, hiding behind a damn ski mask. I hated that Rico even got himself tied up with Chase. I just wished that when Dave and I got out of the game, he did the same. But the nigga was so fucking hard-headed.

The nigga could have done anything with his life. He could have told me he wanted to open a damn daycare to spend more time with all his kids while his baby mommas did their own shit, and I would have told him I would go half on the building and even signed my kids up to go there. But that fast money had the nigga by a chokehold, and now we here.

And the reality is I know my big brother. Chase was the type of nigga that even if Rico came up with the money, Chase would still have his ass off just for the principle of the situation. I just prayed that it wasn't me that Chase sent to do the shit. I was no killer, that was something me and Chase discussed, and the whole time I was in the game, I avoided having to do it. I had shot at a few niggas here and there to show I was no bitch, but it was never to the point of committing murder. "Fuck," I said to myself as I thought of that shit. I had to figure something out.

Rico and I weren't close like we used to be, but in my eyes, once a brother was always a brother, and I couldn't let him go out like that. He had already been through enough. Not to mention how I couldn't look Dave in the eyes, knowing I was behind the shit happening to his cousin. I just didn't know how I was going to make this shit go away. I damn sure didn't want Chase to think I was crossing blood.

As I sat there, my phone rang again. I opened one eye and slid my finger across the screen without even looking at who was calling because I was sure this time it was Traci. "Yeah, babe?" I answered. "Bae?" Brandy's voice said through the phone. "Damn, I'm sorry. I thought you were my girl," I told her as I opened my eyes. "I mean, I could be," Brandy said in a flirty voice. I ignored her statement and asked her what was up.

"Are you busy?" she asked. After last night, I didn't expect to hear from her again, or at least not this soon. "Nah, I'm not busy; what's up?" I said to her, "Well, I've been up all night since you dropped me off studying for this test, and I got to school, and class was canceled. So I figured maybe we could go get some breakfast?" she said.

I was quiet on the phone for a moment. A part of me was telling me to tell her no and send her on her way. But after what Chase had told me and being around her last night, I wanted to get to know her a little better for myself. "Jayden, you there?" she asked. "Yeah, I'm here; where are you trying to go?" I asked her. "It doesn't matter; you pick," she said. "Cool, I got somewhere in mind. Do you need me to pick you up?" I asked her. "Yeah, I'm at the community college if you want to pick me up from here," she told me. "Okay, say less I'll be there in a few," I told her.

As I got up to leave the shop, I had to check myself. "Nigga, you ain't been home all night. You better check the fuck in." I said to myself. I picked up my phone and dialed Tracy's number. "Hey bae," she answered, still sounding half asleep, "hey ma you good?" I asked her. "Yeah, I'm straight. What time is it?" she asked. "Almost 10am " I told her. "Damn, let me get up. What time did you leave this morning?" I looked at the phone, confused.

Tracy must have been drinking last night because she thought I came home last night. Shit, I wasn't about to start a fight if I didn't need to. "I left not too long ago. You were sleeping so peacefully I didn't want to wake you. But I wanted to get down to the shop to make sure everything was good. Then I'm a meetup with Dave and make my way by the laundry mat some time today." I told her. "Okay, well, I'm getting up and getting ready to drop the kids off at camp and then get to the restaurant, so we are open for lunch," she said.

"Okay, I'll be there too," I told her. "Okay, handsome, I love you," she told me. "Love you too, ma," I said back and hung up.

As I made it out of my office and locked up. One of my barber's Trell was coming in. "damn boss what are you doing here already." He asked. "Just handling some shit. But I'm out; hold down the shop." I said to him and went out the door.

I got into my black Mercedes-Benz E-Class and pulled off. As I drove, all I could think about was what the fuck I was doing. I knew Brandy was Chase shorty, and even though he had a wife, there was a code between men and especially brothers, and it was clear I was looking at this girl a little differently now. But shit, there was nothing wrong with at least eating with her and getting to know her a little better.

DAVID

LIFE WAS GOOD. Who would have thought that a light skin nigga from the hood would ever be where I was today. My pops died when I was young, and before he died, he gave my mom and me everything we wanted and needed. When he died, the life insurance went by fast, and my mom did everything she could for me, Jayden and Rico. But I got to the age when I realized I had to do some things for myself to get where I wanted to be. I stayed focused, and I did wrong at times. But everything I did pathed the way for me to be here.

I just wished when I got out of the game, the game would have completely let me go. But shit, here I was getting ready to walk into Attica to talk to one of my clients, who was also my old connect Chase. When this nigga got tied up, I wished he forgot my number, but I owed him. The truth of the matter was I owed him for putting me, Jayden, and Rico on when we were younger, and I owed him because, with all the money he paid, he was about to get me into that spot as the first black partner at my firm.

I opened my briefcase and took my gun out, and put it in my glove box. I took a deep breath and got out of my car. I walked in and flashed my badge when I walked in. The sound of the metal gates closing behind me still bothers me every time I come up here. Jayden and I worked our asses off so this wouldn't be our reality... I wanted to make this meeting quick because the big meeting at the firm was at twelve-thirty. I walked into the private meeting room and took a seat. I looked at my phone, and Amber had sent me a little pic of her before she got dressed. She was getting thick; I guess I was making her happy. I loved that girl. She was the mixture of class, hood, and everything else I needed to balance myself.

As I damn near drooled over her picture, the room door opened, and Chase walked in. This nigga never ceases to amaze me. This dark skin Rick Ross look-alike nigga walked in. There was no handcuff, no uniform, and the latest Jordans on and had the nerve to slap up the guard. I put my phone into my briefcase as he took a seat.

"What's up, Diggy? Tell me you got good news for me." Chase said as the police officer exited the room. "First off, I am your lawyer. My name is Dave or David. Don't call me Diggy; I am not that person anymore," I said to him with a straight face. "Well, damn my bad nigga." He said, laughing. The news I have for you is this. They are offering to move your trail up. Right now, they have one witness, but they are not releasing their information." I told him. "I know who it is," he answered boldly. "Huh? Who is what?" I asked him. "Who the fuck the witness is nigga." he said. I looked through the papers I had in front of me, wondering if I had looked past the paperwork the Feds released with the name of the witness. But it wasn't there. "How do you know that?" I ask him. "We both know it ain't shit I ever wanted me to don't get," he said to me.

Chase was right. I had seen him get everything he wanted and more while I was in the game. "Well, who is it?" I asked him. "Rico!" he said as lean forward on the table. "Rico who?" I asked, hoping it was not the person I was thinking of. "Your mutha fucking cousin." Chase said to me in a tone that sent chills down my body.

My heart dropped, hoping that this shit was wrong. Rico had been locked up for a minute now over some crazy shit. But I know damn well that he did not make a deal with the feds. Rico had always been solid and loyal to the game. You don't snitch no matter what happens; you take what is handed to you and deal with it. I know the shit he was being given lately wasn't the best, but damn I knew damn well he ain't do this shit. "Your damn cousin snitched on me to get the fuck out early and now I'm sitting in here." Every bit of lawyer in me faded away for a moment as I leaned on the table. "Are you sure? And if so, what does that mean?" I said to him, not as his lawyer, but man to man.

"I'm positive I had one source tell me and another source confirm. That nigga is out and in these streets while I'm dealing with this shit. So you know, like I know, he will be dealt with." Chase said. "Now you know I can't let you do shit to my auntie or his kids. Whatever your beef is with Ric, I understand if he did what you said, then by street law, he pays the price. But no one else." "Or what little nigga." he said to me. "Chase, we both know I may have changed for the better; but don't forget that nigga that I used to be that will do whatever, whenever, still lives inside of me." Chase cut me off. "Nigga, be careful what you say. Remember, I can make shit happen," He said with only the left side of his mouth moving. I looked him in the eyes. "Be careful what you do." I told him.

Chase and I were giving each other a stare-down before I finally stood up. "I got to go." I said to him, "Yeah, run and go check on your family. If you know what's best." Chase said with a smirk. "If you knew what was best, you'd play smart, Chase. I am the key to you getting out of here," I said to him as I got my briefcase and walked out. "If you were smart, you'd remember who I am and what I am capable of. Don't think that these walls or that suit can save you. Do your fucking job that I pay you for." He said to me,

I looked him in the eyes for a while, imagining wrapping my hands around his neck and choking him until his lifeless body fell out of the chair with me on top of him. Chase smiled at me. "I know that look, nigga. Do it! We both know I ain't scared to die and this wouldn't be the first life you've taken." He said to me, "difference between you and me. I've changed." I told him, "You changed, or you got good at hiding who you really are? Crazy, you niggas hide more from each other and yall supposed to be brothers." Chase said. I wasn't sure what he meant by that, but I wasn't standing around here to let him play more mind games with me.

"You know Chase's next meeting your new lawyer will be here to meet you. You have a good day and try not to drop the soap nigga." I walked away, and Chase grabbed my arm. "Don't be a dummy. You are my lawyer," he said, looking me in the eye. I looked at his hand on my arm and then back at him before I snatched it away and walked to the door and exited before my thoughts became a reality.

Once I got outside, I called Jayden. His phone went to voicemail after a few rings. "Yo Jay, when you get this shit, call me back." I got to my car and made another call. "Yo," a voice answered that I hadn't heard in a long time. I need something done." I said. "Okay, send me a location for where you want to meet." The voice said and then hung up.

Brandy

I HAD LIED to Jayden about my class being canceled. With everything that happened last night and then coming to school and finding out my school check from Chase hadn't cleared yet, I was in no mood to deal with class. I figured I'd just leave and then fake a doctor's note so my professor would let me retake the test. When a black Mercedes-Benz E-Class with a tint all the way around, pulled up on me at the bus stop, I automatically turned on my attitude. That was, until Jayden rolled down the window and told me to hop in.

He was blasting pop smoke and smoking a blunt when I got in the car. I had to admit his dark skin ass was fine. He wasn't who I wanted, but he was definitely at least eye candy and clearly he got money some how. Chase's bitch Precious had already made it clear she knew all about me when she called me a few days ago. She let me know as long as Chase was locked up; I was on my own. When Chase called me, I cried to him about it, and he told me as long as I did what he said, he would make sure I was good. But I had to be sure. And I had to have a backup plan just in case Chase didn't get out. And last night, Jayden clearly showed me the interest was there; I just see I have to push him to pursue it.

The song changed, and Kevin Gates Me too came on. And Jayden sang along. Heard you want a nigga that's gon' please you.

Suck your toes, dick you down, please you

She says, bae, I'm nasty, I say, me too

Girl, you're addicted, and I need you. I watched his lips as I wondered if he was about that life he was rapping about. As the song ended, I asked. "So you that type of nigga?" but before he could answer, Time today by Moneybagg Yo came on, and I got turned up as my favorite part came on. I don't like niggas; I don't like bitches.

I don't like nobody (nobody, nobody)

We can get gangsta, we can keep it cordial

How do you wanna go about it? "I would ask you if you were that type of chick, but you showed me last night that you are a real gangsta." He said, laughing.

"No, I'm not an angel." I said, playfully punching him. "Shit, fuck you're like a pit bull in a dress. You don't play... but that shit is sexy," Jayden said to me. We drove in silence for a moment before I finally asked him. "So where are you taking me?" "I know this chill little low key spot we can go to, that has dope ass food," he answered. "Low key? Don't want your baby momma to see us?" I asked him. "Listen shorty, I'm only saying this once. My baby mom is nothing you should ever speak about. You don't know her or the relationship I have with her. And she damn sure is not worried about you. So we will not joke or play when it comes to her. Iight?" he said. "Okay," I said.

This nigga was different. Not too many niggas defended their baby momma to the next chick no matter what type of relationship they had or didn't have. Then again, when most niggas are with the next chick, they are trying to fuck. But Jayden wasn't even hinting towards wanting the pussy, and that was odd. I had all types of men tripping over my dark skin sexy ass. My ass was fat; my stomach was flat; my breast sat nice and perky. Not to mention I had my own, and I made stuff happen. Silence came over the car again until Jayden broke it. "So I have a question, and I hope this doesn't offend you." "What's up?" I said to him, "how the hell do you have dark green eyes? I've never seen that shit before on a dark skin girl." He said to me,

I laughed because that wasn't the first time I heard that question. "My dad was white and had green eyes. So I got my mom's skin complexion and his green eyes." I told him. "Okay, so that makes sense why Amber is high yellow." He said to me, I laughed again. "Nah, although that was what my mom told people, so that her good school teacher reputation wouldn't be ruined. Amber's dad is the same color as her. Or at least he was in the pictures we found of him in a box under our mom's bed back in the day." Jayden nodded his head and said nothing. And I couldn't help but wonder if he was judging me by what I just told him.

It wasn't long before we pulled up to an old-looking apartment building. And I looked at Jayden like he had five heads. I knew I lived in the hood, but this was lower than that; there was no way he brought me to this run-down ass building. "What's this?" I asked him with my face frowned up. "relax and just come inside," he said with a smirk as he got out of the car. Every bit of defense popped up in me as I looked at my surroundings, and I wondered if Jayden had told Chase about me kissing him. And if now they were setting me up for crossing lines. Jayden walked around and opened my door. "You coming?" he asked. I hesitated for a moment; then, I finally got out.

We walked up to the building, and Jayden opened the door

for me to walk in. As soon as I stepped in, the smell of piss and god knows what else hit my nose, and my stomach started to hurt, making me want to throw up. Jayden passed me and led the way. I followed him, watching where I stepped and touching nothing at all.

After climbing two flights of stairs and walking down a long hall, I was so happy to see Jayden put his keys in a door because I was tired of holding my breath. All I could do was hope that inside smelled better than in this hallway.

When I stepped into the apartment, everything was different. This was like some shit you've seen in movies or New York City. This nasty-ass building held the most beautiful apartment I've ever seen in my life. It was even up there with the townhouse that Dave and Amber had in the gated community. The smell of piss was washed away and filled with the smell of bleach and febreeze. I looked around, still scared to touch anything or step anywhere because the apartment was covered in white, from the furniture to the throw rugs on the floor. The only place you saw color was the artwork that hung on the walls. There was no way Jayden decorated this place. It was full of glasses, crystals, and things that made this place look straight off a display floor or a magazine.

As I looked around, taking in everything because of the open floor plan, Jayden dropped his keys on the kitchen island. "who's place is this?" I asked. "Mine. Get comfortable. Make yourself at home." He said to me as he headed to the back, taking off his shirt while he was walking. After a few minutes of looking around, I went to the back where he was.

I walked into the bedroom, and the only word that came out of my mouth was "damn." The all-white décor followed into here. A king-size bed with a tufted headboard almost touched the ceiling, and enormous windows made even this rugged part of the city seem beautiful. I took a seat on the bed.

Shortly after, I heard the sound of the shower come on. I looked around the room, trying to find some type of evidence that this was the home Jayden shared with his family. Or if he just used this to flex when he had bitches. But I found nothing.

As I listened to the water run, curiosity got the best of me. I got off the bed, walked over to the bathroom in the room, and pushed the door that Jayden left cracked open. The glass shower was straight in front of me, and I was getting a magnificent view of Jayden's tattooed back and ass. I read the tattoo he had on his back in my head. I'm their keeper and wonder what it meant. He was in great shape, which was a breath of fresh air from Chase's fat ass. "So after you shower we are going to go get food right." I asked as I leaned against the door frame.

Jayden turned and faced me, utterly unbothered by me seeing him naked or his manhood that hung low like a third leg. "I was thinking I could cook up something for us here. I got some food in the fridge," he responded. "You cook, oh lord I'm a die." I said sarcastically, with a laugh. "Don't try to play me. I'm dope as hell in the kitchen. I learned from my mom before she passed away and she could throw down. Everyone in the hood bragged about her food." He said to me, "mmhm," I said back to him.

"I'm for real. You know the restaurant momma way? That's mine. When we first opened, I was the only cook until I found someone that could deliver my mother's recipes the way I wanted." He bragged. "yeah well, we will see." I said. "Yup, well now get your little nasty self out of here trying to peek at my package and let me finish my showering." He said to me, followed by a laugh.

Although I could have said something smart, he was right. All I was trying to do was see what he was working with. Just in case I didn't get to touch it. I went back out to the main area and took a seat on the white sectional. I turned on the big tv that was hanging on the wall. I was well into a movie on the lifetime channel when I heard Jayden's voice from behind me. "I see you made yourself comfortable." He said, making me turn around and damn near drool over his ass as he stood there shirtless in some grey sweats that showed his dick print. I pulled myself together before Jayden saw me looking at his dick print. "ain't that what you told me to do?" I said back to him, turning around on the couch.

I heard Jayden laugh as he went into the kitchen area. "Do you have to be a smart ass all the time?" he asked me. "I'm not being a smart ass; I am just answering your question," I said to him. "Mmhm, I get it," he told me. "Get what?" I said, looking back at him, confused about what he was talking about. "That tough little girl smart mouth shit is your defensive wall you try to put up to protect you, but that little shit doesn't bother me.

I got up off the sectional and walked over to the kitchen area. "You act like you know me or something." I said to him, "I'm figuring you out little by little now." He told me. I leaned on the kitchen island and watched Jayden pull things from the fridge. "So this is your place or just somewhere you bring hoes." I asked him.

"I haven't had hoes in a long time. I am faithful to my girl." He told me, and all the hope I had for getting him left me. "So?" I said, waiting for him to explain. "So this is my home away from home. I used to use it for something else, but I fixed it up. And instead of having a man cave at home like some people, I have this." He said to me, "So you got this place and a place with wifey?" I told him, looking around again, realizing if this was his home away from home. The one he rested his head at on the regular had to be even better.

"yup!" he answered as he cracked some eggs into a bowl he pulled from one of the cabinets. "So if it's not too much to ask, how do you afford all this? You don't seem like the lawyer type like Dave, and you damn sure don't seem like the drug dealer type like Chase." I said to him, "what makes you assume that?" he asked me not to look up from the omelet he was making us. "Because your best friends with Dave can't see him being best friends with a drug dealer unless he keeps you out of jail. And you just don't appear to be the lawyer type." I answered.

"Once upon a time I sold drugs, though, and I was good at it. That drug money actually built the foundation for me to have all of this; my barber shop, the laundry mat, my restaurant, and even this building." He answered me. I was in complete shock. "Really?" I asked him. "Yeah, I grew up just like any other hood kid. No, dad around and mom doing what she can to make things happen. I always knew I had a brother out there on my dad's side, but me and Chase weren't allowed to have a relationship because of our mom's differences. Once our parents were gone, Chase was older and getting to the money. I was still young. But we built a relationship because we were all we had now. The first thing Chase did, though, was put me on. He didn't like my living situation and wanted to ensure I was always good. I just had the right mind to get what I needed and get the fuck out of dodge while I could." He said to me,

"so, does Dave know about your past or Chase?" I asked. "He knows about the drugs, but not that Chase is my brother. I want no one to think Chase only looked out because he was my brother." He said to me, "shit, I wouldn't even care what people thought. I wish I had someone to help me in that type of way." I said. "What do you mean? You got Amber?" Jayden said to me as he added bacon, onions, and green peppers to the food. "Don't be fooled by what you see. It's not always what you see. I choose to communicate with my sister because she is all I have, just like you feel about Chase. But be clear, Amber isn't worried about helping nobody or being there for no one but her damn self.

Jayden nodded his head, and I was sure he probably had multiple questions. Amber painted an impressive picture that she had everything together, but it would mess up her perfect little life if people knew what I knew.

Jayden turned off the stove and looked up at me. "Come over here and try this," he said to me. I walked over and stood next to Jayden. He lifted me up onto the counter next to the stove. He picked up a fork and put some of the omelet on it. And brought it over to me. As seductively as I could, I ate the food off the fork as I looked at him in his eyes.

"I'm glad I'm getting to know you Brandy, you're a dope girl. It's crazy. It took all this for us to be here." He told me. "I agree." I said, looking him up and down. "So what's your story?" he asked me.

No one had ever shown genuine interest like this to me. I looked away from Jayden and he turned my head back to him. "My past doesn't really matter at this point in my life. I'm just trying to have better, you know. Get to where you, Amber, and Dave are. that way I don't always have to feel like the one that works so hard but gets the short end of the stick." I told him. "Is Chase a part of that better?" Jayden asked me as he looked into my eyes. "He's the only person who showed he cared enough to even try to help me." I told him. "Well, how can I show you that I care enough to help?" a piece of me was rejoicing because I had Jayden where I wanted him. But another part of me wanted to just sink into Jayden's arms.

I leaned forward and grabbed Jayden's face like he grabbed mine earlier and kissed him. The kiss we shared last night was a trap, but this one was passionate and instantly made my panties wet. I wrapped my arm around his neck and closed my eyes, and took it all in. I was no longer hungry for food, but I was utterly craving Jayden.

I rubbed my hands down Jayden's chest; I kept my eyes

closed as Jayden moved to my neck and kissed and sucked on it. His lips were so soft. And each touch and lick seemed so perfectly planned out and perfectly placed. That I let out a slight moan. Jayden stopped and looked me in my eyes. As if he was waiting for me to give him some kind of sign. I took his hand and slid it under my shirt, and placed it on my breast. And pulled him back in for another kiss.

He helped me out of my shirt, and then we kissed again before he cupped his hands under my ass and carried me to the bedroom. He placed me on the bed so gently and unbuttoned my jeans I had on. He looked at me with so much amazement before he kissed me again. He eased his hand under me and unsnapped the red bra I had on, and released my breast. I covered them with my hands. For some reason, I was still shy around men I actually liked. He kissed my hands and moved them to my side before telling me to relax. Sex with Jayden was so different from with Chase. He was paying attention to every part of my body, not forgetting to kiss or lick any part. Usually, with Chase after I sucked his dick, it was straight to pound town.

Jayden got to my inner thighs and stopped when he saw the marks and bruises. Before my mom passed, she would abuse me. But to make sure no one saw it, she put marks in places that I kept covered. Usually, no one saw them. I looked down at Jayden and he looked up at me. The shame must have been written all over my face, but instead of asking questions, he kissed my imperfections.

When Jayden pushed my thong to the side and sat his tongue on my pearl, my body melted just like chocolate. It was something about the way he was flicking his tongue. I grabbed Jayden's head and rode his face as he kept my ass cupped in his hands. When I climaxed, he didn't stop until he licked up every drop. When he lifted his head, his lips looked like he had lip-gloss on. And he licked them with a smirk on his face. I sat up and untied his sweatpants and watched them drop to the floor. I went to grab his dick to return the favor and taste his juices, but he pushed my hand and asked me if I wanted it. I nodded my head yes as I bit down on my bottom lip and looked at him. He placed his hand under my chin and told me, "then tell me how to give it to you." Before pushing me back into the bed and climbing on top of me.

DAVE

I HAD BEEN SITTING in my office stressed for about an hour now. That meeting with Chase had played in my mind my entire drive. I had so many questions. If Rico was free, where was he? If he snitched, what murder did he see? And why the hell out of all people would he risk his life and play with Chase.

As soon as I got to my office, the first thing I did was to do some research. And it was true Rico was out of jail and had been for a while now. But the question was, where the fuck was he. This nigga had been a free man for what seemed like six months now, and I hadn't run into him, and he hadn't hit my line. We were supposed to be bros. The least he could have done was put me on to what was going on. I would have never agreed to be Chase's lawyer for this case if I knew.

The more I let my mind fill with questions, the more I got pissed off because it was clear that my auntie did not know he was home. I made it my business to see her a few times a week, and she hadn't mentioned anything, and according to his record, Rico had been home for over six months now. I couldn't possibly think what the hell would keep him from his mother while she was battling stage four breast cancer and had been for the whole three years he was surviving. Auntie needed him, and with Rico getting H.I.V while in jail, I was sure he needed us as a family.

There was a knock at my office door, and then my assistant walked in and handed me a file. When he walked back out, I opened the file and read. Rico's file told me that he was found barely holding on to life in his cell while he was in Attica. After examination, Rico suffered from 3 stab wounds that were infected, four cracked ribs, and H.I.V. the COs concluded that Rico was possibly involved in either an attack or a gang rape. It pissed me off because I knew those C.O. gave no fucks about the black prisoners in that jail and would let anything happen and turn a blind cheek to it, especially if they knew it would track back to them. And with the pride Rico had I was sure he said nothing to nobody about it. I found out about him having H.I.V from my aunt. She said Rico called home crying one day, saying he was dying and when she asked why, he told her.

The file stated that the C.O questioned him multiple times, but he said nothing. But it was to be believed that the father of the victim from the Rico case was housed in Attica and was either involved or called a hit on Rico in revenge for his daughter. "Fuck," I said as I put my head down. At this very moment, I just wanted to know where Rico was just to hug him and see that he was okay. A tear rolled down my face, and I quickly pulled myself together. Rico had it the hardest out of all of us. No, dad at all. Then his mom was an addict who left him with my momma and me. And when she came back and got him, she caused him more stress and pain than she gave him love.

I took a deep breath and went back to reading the file; as I got to the end, all it stated was that Rico was released because of a reason that was sealed and secured by the U.S government. I didn't ever want to think that Rico was a snitch, but from the way things were looking, it looked like Chase was right, and that shit made me uneasy. A lawyer or not, I knew that cops did nothing for you unless they felt like they were getting a win out of it.

Seeing that they had been trying to get Chase for years, and he was now a big fish to them, it would stroke any cop's ego to be the one to say that they took him down. So, of course, they would give Rico his freedom if that meant he would help them get Chase.

If Rico snitched, that meant everybody he loved had a target on them now. And I couldn't let anything happen to Rico's family. I disapproved of him snitching. He would have to face the consequence of that as a man. But I wouldn't let anyone else get hurt behind it.

For some reason, I couldn't help but feel like this was my fault. When Jayden got connected, he came to me with the idea of us making some moves to make money together. He knew how badly I wanted to go to law school, but I didn't want my mom to kill herself, making it happen. I pulled Rico in the game with us because I knew he needed it just as much as we did. And I couldn't imagine getting money and leaving him out.

But when Jayden and I left the game, I saw Rico turn into another person. He was hurt, and I didn't even try to help him. The fact of the matter was we agreed that as long as one was in that lifestyle, we all were. But I basically turned my back on Rico and left. I got what I needed and left him to figure out that lifestyle alone.

As I sat in my office thinking, my cell phone rang. "Hello," I answered. "I just got back into town. I can meet you at that spot if you texted me in twenty minutes." The voice said to me. I looked at my watch and realized it was only 11:30, thanks to them pushing back the meeting for today to 2 pm. I had enough time to make this quick and get back to the office. "Alright on my way." I said. I quickly got up. I grabbed an envelope from my desk drawer, my phone, and keys and headed out of my office.

It took me about fifteen minutes to make it to the meeting spot. I sat in my car missing those days when I smoked because, at this moment, a good blunt would definitely help to smooth this stress; after a few minutes, there was a knock on my passenger window; I hit the lock, and the door opened and Blaze got in. "What's good with ya, boy? Never thought I'd hear your voice on my line again," he said. "Never thought I would have to be on your line again." I told him. "Well, what do you need my guy?" He said. "I need someone's handled," I told him as I turned and looked at him. "And you called me?" he asked. "Yeah nigga," I said, getting annoyed by the dumb-ass question.

Blaze was a hitman and a damn good one at that. His real name was Enrique Cruz. In my first year of college, my mom also got diagnosed with breast cancer; it seemed to run in my family. And was taken out of work. We had some money but not enough, and I was using all the drug money I had on school and being fly. I went to Chase and told him my issue, and he connected me with Blaze. We did hits together, and I walked away with duffle bags full of cash. To this day, Jayden and Rico know nothing about it, and I work my ass off as a lawyer, hoping that the good I do covers the lives I have taken.

Blaze and I didn't cross paths after I changed my life because the nigga didn't need lawyer friends in his corner because he never got caught. He was just that damn good. "Well, who is the person?" Blaze asked me. "Chase," I said boldly. "that fat fuck is in jail." He told me. "And is that going to be a problem?" I asked. "Not at all, as long as you can pay the cost," Blaze said with his hand out. I took the envelope out of my suit jacket pocket and passed it out to him. Blaze opened it and ran his finger over the crisp hundred-dollar bills and then nodded his head. Consider the nigga good as gone. But I do want to know one thing." He said to me, "what?" I answered. "You're just as good as me? Why didn't you save your money and do this shit." He asked me. "Because I defend niggas that commit murder, I can't be out there doing it." I told him. Blaze looked at me and shook his head. "I still think you should have left that lawyer shit alone and did this shit. You were that nigga." He said to me, "That's for your opinion. Now, get out of my car." I told him,

Blaze got out, and I pulled off quickly. I wasn't proud of what I had just done, nor was I fond of the shit I did in the past. There were certain people that I had killed and their faces still popped up in my dreams. Every day I told myself I did what I had to. And this was no different; with Rico being in hiding, I had to handle this. The last thing I wanted was for someone to kill my poor auntie. So I figured if someone took out Chase. Chase couldn't call any hits. And there would be no need for Rico's statement.

I drove back to my office in silence for a while before I picked up the phone and made a call. "Hello," my auntie's voice came through. The weakness I heard in her voice always made me think of my mom and how I watched her go through breast cancer, get her breast removed, and recover. The number of times I literally had to carry them both to bed, watching them in pain as they told me they were okay. It was funny they couldn't stand each other, but they were so much like in so many ways. The only thing is this cancer has changed my auntie a lot. She was sober and very loving.

"Hey, auntie Clara." I said to her, "Hey little boy, how are you?" she said. "I'm okay. But I should ask how are you?" I told her. "I am okay. Pushing through," she told me. "When is your next doctor's appointment or chemo?" I asked her. "I got Chemo in two days and a doctor's appointment in a few weeks," she said to me. "Okay, I will try to clear my schedule to take you, but if not, I will send Amber. Or you can always call my mom, and she can take you. I am sure that she would love to be by your side to help you through this. And even give you some motivation seeing that she went through this too." I said to her, "Baby, you know I love you, but if you send your momma to my front door, I will use the little bit of strength I have to beat your ass." she said.

I laughed. "Sick and still feisty," I told her. "Nah, sick and still real. I don't like that bitch, and just because we both had breast cancer like momma doesn't mean I'm a fake like I like her. If this takes me out, at least people will say I was the same person to the end." she said to me.

"Okay okay lady." I said, letting go of this subject, but I would not stop. I tried all the time to get my mom and auntie back together. They were all they had. But there was so much hate between the two of them that neither of them ever took the time to explain to us why our family was so divided.

Silence took over the phone for a moment, and then my aunt asked, "have you gone to see Rico?" I hesitated before answering, not even sure how to respond. "No, ma'am." I finally said. "I don't know what's going on with you boys, but y'all need to get it together. That way you can help my baby get out of that place and home to me and his kids. It would make me feel so much better if he was home. Just to hug my son. Or to sit and talk to him one last time. I feel like I could leave this earth after having those last moments with him," she said to me. At that moment, anger came over me, and I was debating on telling my auntie Clara that Rico had been released from jail for months now, but I changed my mind. She was already hurting, and I had no authority to break her heart in that way. "Auntie, don't talk that way." I said to her, "I'm just being honest baby." she said to me. "Okay auntie, well I'm pulling up to work. I will check on you later. Have any bills you need me to pay out and ready for me." I told her.

Brandy

"WHAT DO you think Chase will say when he finds out about this?" I asked him. "I'm not sure, but I am going to go see him this afternoon." Jayden said. "To tell him about this?" I asked, as I jumped up. Jayden laughed. "No, I am going to just go check on him. And tell him what happened last night. Relax. If you want to keep us a secret, we can. I got shit to lose just like you." he must have noticed the look on my face as he told me that.

I laid back on his chest and shook my head. "What's all that about?" he asked me. "I just get tired sometimes of being the best kept secret. Men like you never pick me." I told her. "What is that supposed to mean?" Jayden said as he placed his hand under my chin and made me look up at him. "Nothing," I said, moving my head away and then moving my whole body to the other side of the bed and pulling the covers around me.

"Man, listen, I'm not one of them niggas that going to beg you to open up to me. But I'm also not one of them niggas that's going to be cold-hearted and not pick up on the hints you are throwing. Just like Im not going to pretend like I didn't see the marks on your thighs. So if you got something to say, get that shit off your chest, because I'm not asking again and I won't care later." He said to me,

"It doesn't even matter if you won't care." I said to him, "If I didn't care, I wouldn't have said anything. Don't assume you are too beautiful and too smart to do that and make a fool of yourself." I looked into Jayden's eyes, and something just seemed so safe and so genuine. I sat up in the bed and turned towards him.

"Don't judge me please." I said to him, "I am in bed with my brother's girl. I have broken all types of bro code rules. I am the last one to judge anyone at this moment. Believe it or not. I like you." He said. My heart was filled with joy. I had never had a man tell me that he actually liked me, and I was in my damn twenties. "Well, it's just that all my life I have felt like I wasn't enough. So I go harder to be smarter, be sexier, to be better all in all." I said. "Why don't you feel like you aren't good enough." he asked me. "Look at me? Then look at someone like Amber. I'm always compared to her. And no matter how much I try, she does nothing and gets everything my heart desires. Not to mention I've never had anyone that took the time out to build me up. Those scars that you saw are from my mom. When we were younger. She used to beat on Amber. When Amber ran away I became her punching bag. That was until she died. So I've never had it easy. Nothing was just handed to me. Somehow some way I worked hard and sacrified for everything I have.`` I told him.

"What does your heart desire?" Jayden asked me. "Wealth, love, to be taken away from the hood." I told him, trying to fight back the tears. "What you desire is not too much, but you first have to stop comparing yourself to your sister. Is she pretty? Yes. But if you ask me, something is off with the bitch. You are fine and making shit happen for your damn self. You have goals and are driven," Jayden said. Everything in me wanted to scream out, yeah, she is playing your best friend. She fucking on the dude that we just pulled up on last night. But I kept my mouth closed. Because although I indirectly threw her in this shit the previous night being petty, I didn't want any of this heat; Chase was sending Rico's way to hit my sister's front doorstep.

No matter how much I didn't like my sister. I still loved her and wanted no harm to happen to her. "Listen, Brandy; you're a rare find. No kids, you are actually trying to make something happen for yourself instead of using your pussy to get it. I love my girl, but even she doesn't have the drive and determination you have. I respect you, and because of that just I will always be in your corner. But nothing I say matters if you don't see the unique person you are for your damn self.

Brandy

THE SEX with Brany was terrific. After three rounds and that talk with her, I was actually sexually fulfilled and tired. We both passed out and went to sleep. A few hours later, I was awoken and watched Brandy sleep for a while just thinking of the things she had shared with me. It took a fucked up person to abuse their own kids. I felt like that was why I always had a weak spot for Rico cause I seen how his mom mentally fucked him up.

I started to move in the bed and on the tv. Brany rolled over and looked at me. "Did I wake you?" i asked. "It doesn't matter." she told me. "Yes, it does. You were looking so peaceful. It looked like you haven't gotten a good night's sleep like this in a while." I said to her.

Brandy didn't say much she looked like she was in a daze. "You good?" I asked, pulling her in and letting her lay her head on my shoulder. "Yeah, just a lot on my mind." she told me. "Well, tell me about it." I said. "Nah I rather not...." she told me. and I respected her and didn't push the issue; I wanted her to feel free to talk to me openingly when she was ready. For now I was happy with the information that she had shared with me. i just flipped through the channels on the tv that was hanging from the ceiling.

Although I didn't want to leave my apartment, I eventually got up and took Brandy home, and hopped on the road to go see Chase. As I drove, I noticed I had a missed call and voicemail from Dave. I missed the voicemail and made a mental note to call him back when I got out on this visit, seeing that I was already cutting it close. They stopped letting people in at 1:30 pm, and visits ended at 3:30 pm, and it was a long process to get to the visitor room since I wasn't a lawyer like Dave.

Every time I pulled into this place, it was like a grey cloud was around it, no matter how sunny it was out. I mean, think about it, the jail was right next to the damn cemetery. It was like this was a reminder that they didn't plan to free people from here. They wanted you to go from the cell to the damn ground. That shit sucked because outside of Chase, I knew it was nigga up in here that didn't deserve that. They were just dealt a bad hand. It was way more shady niggas out in the world that deserved to be behind these walls in place of the good ones that were in here.

As I sat in my car in the parking lot, I waited for the shuttle to pick me up to take me to the visitor center. When it pulled up, I got out of my car and hopped in. I'm not too fond of these visits because they made you feel like you were in jail, too. You couldn't have your phone, no jewelry, and you had to make sure your clothes could not be something these niggas refused the visit over.

I made it to the visitor center, and they checked me in, reminding me that any phone or other things that weren't allowed in the jail needed to be locked in a locker there. Once I got past that, you got back on the shuttle that took you around the prison to the entrance. Looking out the window at this place to a kid, it would seem like a castle. But to an adult, you knew their walls were to keep people in and caged, not to honor royalty.

Once they got me in, took my picture, made me go through metal detectors, and checked me all the way down to my socks. They stamped my hand, and I went from the main building to the next one behind it. I was listening to the sounds of the gates closing behind me. When I finally got to my seat in the visitor's room, I looked around as I waited for Chase.

I thought it was evil that the visiting room had pictures of cartoon characters painted on the walls. This wasn't a happy place where people wanted to bring children to see their loved ones.

As I sat there, I thought about when Dave and I sat here almost two years ago, waiting to see Rico. This nigga was so mad at us and hated us so much that he refused to leave his cell and come down to the visit. To have the police walk up and tell us that the visit was over before it even started because Rico refused to come down reminded me that he really didn't think we were family anymore.

My thoughts were broken when Chase finally entered the visitor's room. He paid no attention to the C.Os and came over and addressed me. The C.O.s said nothing to him and let him do as he pleased. "Nigga, you ain't been in here long enough to have these damn guards scared." I said to him as we took a seat. Chase laughed. "Nigga, money makes shit happen. I came in here and made it clear who I was and I paid who I needed to, so I can move how I want to. Believe me, these crackers hate my black ass. But money talks." He said to me,

"So what's up? What did you need me to come up here for?" I asked him. "First off, I need you to go by my house and talk to my crazy ass baby momma. She tripping. Not taking my calls or writing to me back on JPay. And Brandy said she reached out to her. If that bitch thinks because I'm locked up, she is untouchable or about to run off with my kids and my money, she has another thing coming. This is just recess for me. That nigga Dave going to get me out of here." Chase told me.

I nodded my head. "Has Dave been up here to see you?" I asked. "Yeah, he was actually up here today. But I don't think he likes the information I gave him." Chase said. "What information did you give him?" I asked. "That his mutha fucking cousin is a snitch." Chase said, putting his hands on the table and leaning toward me. "Why the fuck would you do that?" I asked him.

Because the nigga needed to know. Just in case you and Brandy didn't get the message through Rico's head and make his ass scared, I know his cousin will." Chase said with this crazy ass look on his face. It was moments like this that I thought that Chase's ass deserved to be in here with these mutha fuckers. "That's his cousin, though, and Dave is your lawyer and has been loyal. What the fuck happens to certain things and people being off-limits and having lines you just wouldn't cross with this street shit." I said to him,

"Lines were crossed when I ended up in here behind that nigga. Ain't my fault the nigga got caught up getting a under age bitch high and fucking her. His ass should of did his mutha fucking time and kept my name and business out of his mouth." Chase said to me. "But Chase." I said. Chase got loud, "ain't no fucking but." At that moment, I didn't feel like a grown man sitting at that table; I felt like a little ass kid. "I put money in that nigga pocket, and food in his kid's mouth he should of never crossed me. And you better not sit here and defend him because the nigga only got near me because of you. And the only reason I'm not on your ass because you're my baby brother." Chase said.

"Baby brother or not, I am a grown man and you will not sit here and threaten me or make me feel you're saving me from shit. I told you I was getting out of the game and so was Dave. You could have told Rico no, you were supplying him with shit else. You decided to still work with him. Which led to him even having some shit to give that little girl and this shit unfolding. So miss me with the bullshit because you need me." I said to him,

Chase laughed. "Nigga, I don't need you!" he said to me. "So what was last night then?" I asked him. "Like I told you, nigga, I don't need you. What I had you and Brandy do last night, I could have skipped. I just like my prey to know I am coming for them so that it mentally fucks with them." he said. "So you got that man breaking his neck to get you money just to torture him?" I said, trying to understand Chase's thinking. "Let me be clear whether or not Rico comes up with the money; he's a dead man walking," Chase said as he leaned on the table and looked at me as he whispered the words.

Amber

I MADE it to the bridal store just in time for my dress fitting. But as soon as I walked in, I was greeted with Ms. Dorothie giving me a disapproving face and her legs and arms crossed. "Do you not know that people's time is valuable? Or do you just not care? This young lady has other clients besides you. And I got other stuff I could spend my time doing. I don't do this running on black people time, ghetto stuff. She barked at me. One thing I hated was that Ms. Dorothie was so stuck up. She is acting like she wasn't black and Hispanic. Hell, she acted like she wasn't from the hood too. The only reason she lived how she did now was because of Dave.

"Ms. Dorthie, it's 1pm on the dot. My appointment is for 1pm." I told her as I looked down at my apple watch, checking the time. "1pm does not mean you walk in the doors at 1pm. You should have been here ten minutes early and ready to go. And what do you have on? We are in a high-class neighborhood. Why do you have on this skin tight dress with your breast out? I hope this is not how you dress when my son has you around his colleges." Ms. Dorthie said, as she stood up and put her hands on her hips.

I looked down at my sundress. There was utterly nothing wrong with it seeing that it was over 80 degrees outside, and after being with Rico, it was the simple thing just to throw on and go. Hell, to me, it was better than the outfit I had on when I was creeping to go see Rico. In my head, I was screaming, shut the fuck up. And it must have been written all over my face that I was ready to go off on my future mother-in-law because my childhood friend Courtney stepped in. "Ms. Lott, it is okay! Amber, let me take you back to see your dress. I've put the beads and stones on it like you wanted. Courtney said as she guided me towards the fitting room. "Thank you," I whispered to her. "Don't worry about it. I have a mother-in-law from hell, too. And just so you know, she hating; you wearing the hell out of that dress she just mad because she can't do it." Courtney said to me as she opened the door to the fitting room, and I walked in smiling. At least I knew now I wasn't the only one whose mother-in-law put them through hell.

I got undressed and sat waiting for Courtney to come back. I knew she was going to take a few minutes because she had to get Ms. Dorothie into a fitting room too and then pull both of our dresses that I had her custom make. I figured since I was waiting, I would shoot Dave a text. Bae, I just don't get it; we haven't even been here for two minutes, and your mom is already at my neck. I sent the message to him with the crying emoji.

As I waited for Courtney to come back or Dave to respond, I heard Ms. Dorothie in the fitting room next to me. "David, this is your mother. Call me back ASAP! I don't know who this little girl thinks she is, but I will not stand for the way she is behaving or the way she talks to me. We have a standard to uphold and I will not let her tear it apart." I heard her say, and I rolled my eyes. She was so overdramatic, and she had been trying to get Dave to leave me since we got together.

It was silent for a few, and then I heard Ms. Dorothie's voice again. "Hello? Hey Martha girl. What are you doing? Okay, that's good because I need someone to talk to because this high yellow little girl is trying me. I'm so over this. I don't even know why I agreed to come to this fitting because I am going to use everything I got to make sure my son doesn't marry this girl because she is not the one. I can see it."

I listened closely, wondering if Ms. Dorthie knew how thin these walls were. Ms. Dorthie kept talking. "The girl is worthless. She brings no benefit to my son's life, and she doesn't even try to have a relationship with me. She's just a gold digger. I can see the signs all over her. She is only around because my son is paid. But I will die before I just watched someone like her use and hurt my son. But my son loves her. He pays all the bills while she sits at his house and does nothing. Dave says she cooks and cleans, but I raised him to be self-sufficient so that boy can cook and clean. He doesn't need a little girl just sitting in his house. I just can't take this, Martha. This girl just ain't shit, and I am trying to save my baby from messing up his life behind this girl. But he always got an excuse. He loves her. She's going through a lot because of her mom not being around and then dying. But when I met her sister, she was the total opposite. The girl is in school; she works, has her own place. She would be a way better fit for my son than this girl. I don't even know why I am at this fitting because if it takes the last bit of air in my body, there will be no wedding.

Tears formed in my eyes because I hated being judged by Ms. Dorothie. This woman knew nothing about me, who I was or what I had been through. I didn't work because I had no fundamental skills and just a high school diploma. When I met Dave, I was a bartender. My pretty face and nice body helped me get good tips, and I lived pretty well. It wasn't how I live now, but I was maintaining. When Dave came along, he didn't like the late hours or the way guys would look at me or talk to me, so he told me as long as I was with him. I didn't need to do anything but take care of him as a woman should.

As tears rolled down my face all I could think was how this woman complained I didn't try to have a relationship with her but she never really opened up for me to do so. This hate she had reminded me so much of my mother to the point that it made my stomach hurt, and I felt like I had to throw up.

"*Amber, I know one thing you ain't going to be shit just like your ain't shit daddy.*" *My mom said as she sat at the kitchen table drinking her tequila. I stood at the kitchen sink with my back to her washing dishes, trying to ignore her and the statements that I heard her say repeatedly.* "*you the one that laid down with him and made me.*" *I said under my breath.*

"*What the fuck you say?*" *she yelled.* "*Nothing, ma'am,*" *I said quickly because the last thing I wanted was her to get up out of that chair.* "*You better watch what you say to me little girl because at any time you think you are big and bad enough to talk back to me. We can go outside. And I'm a show you that I am the H.B.I.C in this house and then you can get the fuck out.*" *She said,*

Like any sixteen-year-old, I always said that I couldn't wait to leave my momma, especially with how to mean she was, but I knew for sure I wasn't ready for the world out there if her words still broke me down. I couldn't understand how a woman was around children all day because she was a teacher. She could then come home and be downright out, mean, nasty and hateful to her own child.

I looked up from the sink and locked eyes with Brandy, who was peeking her head into the kitchen. Momma never treated her how she treated me. "*Brandy, go find yourself a damn seat. Ain't nothing in here for you.*" *My mom yelled out to her. I looked at my sister, and although she was the younger one, my eyes were crying out for her to save me. She gave me a sad look.* "Now Brandy!" *my mom yelled before Brandy walked away.* "Amber, why is it taking your dumb ass so long to finish washing those dishes." *She asked. I looked at the counter full of pots, pans, and dishes that my mom had pulled out the cabinets in a drunken rage and demanded I wash when we got home from school.*

"Momma, I am moving as fast as I can." *I told her.* "If these dishes were some dick, your little fast ass would rush through them. Wash my damn dishes with the same energy you had when you were in that little boy's face while my baby was fighting and you weren't trying to help her. With your selfish ass." *I didn't understand any of this. Brandy was fighting after school, but I was in trouble. It wasn't my fault that Brandy's temper was just like mama's, and it went from zero to a hundred. And the boy she was accusing me of being in his face was our neighbor Kevin. Momma swore up and down that Kevin and I were doing something. But I didn't let anyone touch me in that way. Not after her last little friend, Mr. Robert, raped me, and then she told me I was a liar when I told her.*

"Hurry up Amber." *My mom said from behind me.* "I am momma." *I cried out with my hands shaking as I washed the dishes because I knew this could quickly go left over something this small, especially because she was halfway through a freshly opened bottle of tequila.*

As I used my forearm to wipe a few tears that had run down my face, the glass that momma was drinking from flew by, my head just missing me and shattered on the wall behind the sink. I spun around and looked at her with my eyes big as she grabbed another cup and poured a fresh drink like she hadn't done anything. "You better wash them dishes and stop looking at me like that." *She told me. I turned back to the sink and tried to clean up the broken glass.* "I can't wait to be away from all this craziness." I said under my breath seconds later; I felt a sharp pain in the back of my head and heard the sound of glass breaking. I fell to the floor, hitting my head on the sink on my way down.

My mom stood over me and kicked me as I rolled over in pain, holding my head. "I told you your smart ass mouth was going to get your ass beat. Now look. Your dumb ass done made me waste my bottle." She said as I heard Brandy's footsteps rushing towards me. "Momma, what did you do? Her forehead is bleeding." Brandy said as she looked at me over and over in my hands. I looked up at my mom, and she looked at me with disgust and gave a slight sound, and then said to me, "shit now you can't take your dumb ass to school." She told me. Then she stepped over me and walked out of the kitchen like I was nothing.

I came back to reality when I heard the knock at the dressing room door. Courtney walked in with the black garment bag containing my wedding dress. She hung it up and then unzipped the bag. And the shine from the stones and beads that covered the heart-shaped top of my dress was the first thing I saw.

Courtney helped me into the dress, and once I was in it, I adored the way it shaped my body and how it looked as I looked down at it. I looked at Courtney, and she dropped a tear. "You okay?" I asked her. "Yeah, it's just five years in this business and knowing where we came from; you look amazing Amber." She said, wiping her eyes. "Do I?" I said. "Let's go see it, girl." She said, opening the door. We walked out to the showing room so I could see myself in the enormous mirrors. When I stepped on the stage and seemed myself, I covered my mouth in shock. I looked way better than I ever thought I would. Courtney walked up behind me and placed a wedding veil on my head. The tears came streaming down my eyes.

My emotional moment was interupeted by the sound of Ms. Dorthie's voice. "I don't like it." I heard her yell. When she came into the showing room, I wanted to scream out in laughter. Now I couldn't cuss out Ms. Dorthie like I wanted to, but this was a great way to get back. The peach-colored mother of the groom dress I picked out for Ms. Dorthie was just as ugly as I wanted it to be. It had no shape to it at all, and it covered from her neck to her ankles. If I could have figured out a way for it to cover her mouth, I would have done just that.

"you picked this ugly dress out on purpose," she said, walking up to me. "Ms. Dorothie, I picked out a dress that went with the white, peach and gold color theme we had. Plus, I wanted it to be age appropriate, nothing like the unaccept stuff that I wear." I told her smile. "Little girl, I don't know what games you think you 're playing, but I am not the one. I am calling my son. I'm not wearing this." She said as she turned and stormed off back to her dressing room. When she was gone, I turned and looked at Courtney, and she had her hand covering this smile she had on her face. I turned back to the mirror and laughed to myself. "Check mate," I said silently.

RICO

AFTER THAT SESSION WITH AMBER, I got a call on that flip phone, and my mind went into overdrive, and I spent a reasonable amount of time riding around just trying to think things out. It still amazed me that this was my life. If I were still hustling, $50,000 would have been nothing for me to get. But hustling was what got me into this shit. I still remember how everything went down after Jayden, Dave, and I got into it. I went to see Chase because I was going to make shit happen for myself, no matter what.

"Yo Chase, can I talk to you?" I said into my phone when he answered. "Yeah pull up." He told me. I was only five minutes away, and it took me no time to get there. When I pulled up, Chase was sitting in his Range Rover, smoking a blunt. I parked my car and got out. "Take a ride with me." Chase said, pulling off and handing me the blunt. With no second-guessing, I hit the blunt and went for the ride.

"So what do you need to talk to me about?" Chase asked. "So Jayden and Dave want out. I'm not sure if they talked to you about this or not, but I wanted to see how that would affect busi-

ness for you because...." Chase stopped me. "*Do you think you can handle business without them?*" "*Yes,*" I said back quickly. "*Then why are you talking to me about what the next nigga wants to do with his life? You are a grown ass man with your own life and own shit to handle. What Dave and Jayden do is not guaranteed to make sure you're good, so you have to make sure you look out for you.*" Chase said to me. "*You're right,*" I said to him as we pulled up to this apartment building. "*You know what? I'm putting you to the test. Get out,*" Chase said.

We got out of the car and headed into the apartment building. "Knock," Chase said as he reached behind him and pulled his Glock 19 out, and stood at the side of the door, leaning against the wall. I knocked on the door. "Who is it?" I heard a voice say from the other side. I stood there and said nothing. It was a few more moments before I heard the door open. "Can I help you?" This light skin nigga with braids and glasses asked me. "Nah, but you damn sure can help me." Chase said, stepping forward. I watched as the fear came over the nigga's face as he looked at Chase and then down at the gun in his hands.

"*Chase,*" *the nigga said as he backed up with his hands up. Chase walked into the apartment, now raising his gun, and I followed behind him. Making sure no one was watching before I closed the apartment door. "Kameron, you really thought you could owe me money and hide?" Chase asks. "Chase, listen, let me explain. I wasn't hiding from you. I was just here, taking care of my grandmom. She's dying. She is right in the other room." The nigga pleaded. I took a few steps and looked around the wall into one of the rooms. I saw a woman who appeared to be asleep, attached to different machines lying in bed.*

"*Your sad story is not my business. I am worried about my money. So do you have it." Chase asked. "I don't have the whole thing, but I have $5000," Kameron said, pulling the money from* his pocket and holding it up to Chase. Chase slapped the money out of his hand. "Nigga, you owe me $5,000 what the fuck am I going to do with $5,000," chase said real sternly.

"Chase, man, listen. Give me some time maybe a week or two to get something figured out. I'll get you your money, I promise." he said with his voice shaking. "See, had you come to me as a man and told me you were short and needed more time and that ya grandma was doing badly, I would have understood and been happy to do that. I'm human and I love my grandma shit. She raised me... But you, you fucked up and pulled a scary nigga move. You went missing and hiding and made me come looking for your dumb ass. Now i'm not sure if I can even trust you." Chase said, still pointing his gun directly at this nigga.

"Chase, you can trust me, I promise," he said. "Rico, what do you think Chase asked me. I looked at the nigga for a while, understanding that situation he was in and the fear that was running through him. I had to admit I felt sorry for him. But this came with life. We all understood that no matter what happened you made sure you had the money to pay for the product. I looked at Chase, who was staring at me, and finally said. "Trust is all men have between each other. If he fucked that up and you trust him again and give him another chance, if he fucks up again, that's your fault, and shame on you for even giving him that opportunity to play with you like that.

Chase nodded his head as he bit down on his bottom lip like he was thinking. "You know what nigga, you smart." chase said before turning back to the nigga and letting off two shots into him. Living in the hood, we heard about people dying, but I had never been this close to a dead body until now. The surprised look on the old boy's face as he laid on the floor bleeding out made my heart sink. It was crazy; it took that one moment to get on Chase's good side. He even fronted me for my first pack.

But I never expected it. Three weeks later, what was supposed to be a regular traffic stop for me speeding turned into me getting arrested. I had no trap house or place where I felt comfortable leaving my product, so I had it all in my car.

"Inmate, you got twenty minutes to use the phone," the guard said to me as we approached the phones. I picked up the phone and dialed the first number I could think of. *You've reached David. Unfortunately, I am unable to take your call at this time. Please leave your name, your number, and a brief message, and I'll get back to you as soon as possible... beep...* "Dave, it's Rico. I need you, bruh. I'm downtown in jail." I said, then hung up. *The fuck, man,* I picked up the phone again and dialed another number. *You have a collect call from "Remario Piers"* a few moments later a familiar voice came through the phone. "Rico, what's going on," Jay said, and I was so grateful at that moment that despite the beef me and Jay had; he still answered. "Jay, I need your help they got me downtown, Dave not answering I don't have a lawyer I need to get out of here." I said, "what did they pick you up for?" he asked. "I was in the car with this Rican bitch I met at the club, and I was speeding while she was sucking my dick. When they pulled me over, I had the product in the car, and they said the girl was 16 and she was high off my product." I told him.

"I knew some shit like this would happen when you were in the game alone." Jayden said. "Man, it's not the time for that. I told you so bro I need your help." I said, frustrated. "Well, I don't know what to tell you Dave on a trip with his chick in Jamaica, so I cannot reach out to him until he touch down; I have no help to give. I tried to help you avoid this, but you wanted to live this life now you got to deal with what comes with it. I'll tell Dave you are looking for him peace Rico." Jayden said before hanging up on me.

I finally pulled up to my house and got out of the car, preparing myself to hear more of Toni's mouth. I strolled up to the door and stuck my key in the door. When I turned the knob, the door was stopped by the chain Toni had on the door. "Yo Toni" I yelled. Through the small opening, I saw Toni appear and stand with her arms crossed. "What do you want, Remario?" she asked. "Open the doorman. I need to lay down." I told her. "Nah," Toni said. "Man, does it look like I'm fucking playing with you, I paid for this house so girl opens this door," I told her, trying not to lose my cool. "Romario gets off my doorstep, You may have paid for me to get this house but I've been paying to keep it since you been gone." she told me. "Bitch, I live here; now open the door before I kick this shit in. you pissing me the fuck off," I told her.

"Romario, I don't give a damn, just like you didn't give a damn to tell me the truth." She screamed." What the fuck are you talking about," I asked her, confused. "Your ass is out here keeping secrets, so I did some research. Your ass wasn't in jail just for drugs; you're a damn pedophile. And you got H.I.V! And I got you around my damn kids." she said. "Toni, watch your mouth, my kids in that house, I'm not a damn pedophile; I don't touch on kids. And Correction those are OUR KIDS" I told her, "No, you just get them high as hell and let them suck your dick. You're a sorry excuse for a man; you got three baby mommas. We weren't enough for you; you had to go get someone's daughter. And let me guess, since it was no little girls in jail to touch on, you were in there fucking the young, down low boys. I can't believe I let you in my house. And your ass put that infected dick in me and said nothing. So since your life is fucked up, you fuck up mine." She said to me,

I kicked the door. "Toni, let me in the house so we can talk because you don't know what the fuck you're talking about." I said to her, "Mommy is that daddy?" I heard my son say. And I instantly felt like I was in fucking baby boy. "Toni, at least let me see my kids," I told her. "Romario, me and my kids don't need you." My heart broke hearing her say that. I turned and placed my back on the house and slid down onto the ground. "Toni, I need y'all. I need my kids." I said.

As the words rolled off my lips, I noticed a black truck creeping up, and as the windows rolled down, I saw the guns coming out the windows. "Toni, get down." I screamed as the bullets started the ring out. And although I knew the drive-by was quick, it seemed like the shot rang out for so long as I laid on the porch covering my head.

Once I heard the shots stop and the car sped off, I got up. "Toni?" I said as I looked through the cracks of the door. Toni let out a scream, but I couldn't see her or the kids. "Oh, my god!" she said. "Toni, are you okay?" I said, but she didn't respond. I could just hear her and my daughter crying. I backed up and kicked the door in with all my might.

When the door flew open, I saw Toni rocking with my son in her arms as she rocked back and forth. "This is all your fault!" Toni said to me as tears ran down her face. "Baby, I didn't mean for this to happen. I promise. I would never put you guys in danger. I love you." I said to her as I tried to kneel down and touch her. "But you did Rico, you did.... Don't fucking touch me! Call 911." she said to me. I pulled out my phone and dialed 911.

"911, what's your emergency?"

"My son has been shot," I responded.

"Where was he shot?" the operator asked.

"We were at home. A drive-by happened. All I see is blood on his right side, "I told her.

"Okay, 96 South Mitchell street the address." the operator asked me.

"Yes!" I answered, with tears in my eyes.

"Okay sir, hang on, help is on the way." She told me.

I looked down at Toni, and she looked up at me. "If my son dies, I promise you won't have to worry about Chase. I will kill you myself." Toni said to me.

Amber

I WAS SITTING in a women's empowerment meeting when the lady leading the discussion called me out. "Amber, what's your story? Tell us why you're here." I sat there in silence for a moment. Then I finally spoke and said," well, I'm dating Mr. Right, but I'm in love with Mr. Wrong.

The entire room looked at me, and then I realized how crazy what I just said sounded. But hell, it was my truth. I was dating Dave, and things were good. He was a knight in shining armor. He was everything I had dreamed of; he was confident, courageous; he listened to me when I talked; he paid attention to details; he was humble, and he was a well-respected lawyer. I had a love for him; I mean, we had been together for a few years now, and we lived together. But I had to admit, I didn't truly love him. If I did, I wouldn't step out on him from time to time with Rico.

Now, Rico, I loved his ass, and I was in love with his ass; in the words of Ms. Mary J Blige, I love my Mr. Wrong. I met Rico in the club one night when Dave was out of town on business. I needed to let down my hair and not pretend to be perfect like I usually had to do when Dave and I went out. So I took that time to do just that. My sister Brandy and I got dressed and went right to the hood to let loose.

Rico wasn't my regular pick, but something about him pulled me into him. After six months of messing around, finding out about his multiple kids and baby moms, his name and rep in the streets, and his anger and control issues, I'm still here holding on to him.

The lady sitting to the left of me asked, "So why are you here?" I looked at her, wondering why she was all up in my business. And then I sat silent; the honest answer was because I was tired of living a double life. I was lying to both guys and honestly felt like I was on my way to getting caught. I mean, I could only keep telling Dave I was with Brandy, or Brandy had my car so many more times before he ran into her, and she blew my cover, and it would be no one's fault but my own. Or worse, he sees Rico driving my car that is insured in Dave's name, and Dave pays the car note for it.

But I wasn't about to tell these hoes that; I wasn't about to just air my dirty laundry completely out to these women. So, I flashed my ring and said, "Well, my Mr. Right proposed. But I can't leave my Mr. Wrong alone." "Why not?" the same girl asked. I gave her the stare of death because she was all up in my business. "Honestly, my lady box screams out for him," I answered her, trying not to be too nasty with my words. Rico makes love to me in a way that Dave doesn't. He's down for it whenever and wherever; in the car, in the park, 69 or anal. I looked around the room to see the ladies' reactions. They all had facial expressions that let me know that they weren't judging me or what I was saying.

Now don't get me wrong, Mr. Right was packing, and he had a good stroke game. But everything was so routine and predictable. At home, in the bed with the lights off. Mainly in the missionary position, and about 10 or 15 strokes. And he was good. He was never willing to change up to or take a risk. All I wanted was for him to lose control a little bit.

That's why he and Rico were so different. Shit, that's why I felt like I needed Rico; he was everything Dave wasn't. The two of them were like night and day. And although the night was a little scary, I loved the thrill it brought. But we all know you can't live in the nightlife forever. So, it was the time that I prepared myself for the light of day.

The meeting progressed, and I listened to these ladies' stories. When the meeting let out, I drove home thinking of all the things I had heard. Some had been head over hills for some men, and others had hit their lowest point trying to keep a man. It was just more of a sign that I needed to get it together, and quickly.

It's crazy how I can still remember the exact night Rico came into my life. *"Amber, where are you taking us?" Brandy asked in a complaining voice from the passenger seat. "Relax, we're going out to have some fun." I said to her, smiling. "But why? I could be home studying and I know Dave is at home waiting for you. So why?" she said to me. I took a deep breath, trying not to let her kill my vibe. "Brandy, all you do is sit in that apartment and study. You need some fun in your life. You are becoming stuck up," I said to her as I glanced over at her. "No, I need to study. We all can't be like you and get a fine ass, rich, black man to snatch us up and out the hood." She said to me,*

It was so annoying to hear my sister speak like that. She thought my life was perfect because I had Dave. But in all reality, I was tired of being with him. "Brandy, just relax; you're already in the car, so we are going to go have fun. One night out with your big sister won't stop you from being the bomb-ass nurse I know you will be." I told her. "Yeah, okay," she said as she looked out the window. I kept driving to the destination.

"promise me one thing Amber." She said in a real serious

voice. I looked over at her. "What's that?" I asked. "You won't be all over any guys tonight." She said, "That's the fun part. I can't help it that men see me and just want to give me their attention." I told her with a laugh.

"Amber," she said, "what?" I responded. "When are you going to stop, You have a dope ass man at home? He has a good ass job as a lawyer. He provides for you so good that you don't want or need anything. He loves you so much Stevie Wonder could see it. I don't get why you want to go to these nasty ass clubs with these hood niggas that won't do half the shit Dave does for you and disrespect that man, and your damn self. Not to mention pull me in the bullshit and make me guilty by association. When everything you possibly need is right at home waiting for you." She said,

"The good life is boring, Brandy. Do I love the life I live; yes. But sometimes I need more. Sometimes I need something different. Sometimes I need not to be the perfect vision of myself to fit into Dave's world but to let go and remember who I am." I told her. "Okay, understand. Sometimes we all need to go back to our roots here and there but damn it, have some damn kool-aid and sit and think about how blessed you are." Brandy said to me. "Listen, you have your plan on how you are going to get out of the hood. Dave was way out, and I'm thankful for him. But as a woman, I'm not fulfilled. He does not satisfy me. I told her. Brandy shook her head. "Then leave him." She said, "And that would be the dumbest shit I ever did. I leave him and then do what? Come back to the hood and hope that someone comes along again and snatches me up. And theis times hope they know how to fuck my damn brains out. Yeah, I'm not doing that shit." I told her,

Brandy still shook her head. "What?" I asked. "So he doesn't satisfy you sexually and you don't want to leave. Well, teach the man instead of playing with him. Like, do you sleep with these *other men that I see you flirting with in the club?"* She asked me. *"I'm not teaching a grown ass man how to make love to me. At this age, either you got it or you don't. and No, i'm not fucking these niggas. They are just great eye candy to think about when I'm masterbating."* I told her. *"You know there are women dying for a man like the one you are taking for granted. You should feel bad. He asked you to be his wife. You said yes. So are you going to still be doing this shit once you're his wife?"* She asked me.

I took a deep breath. I hated that the hood hadn't stolen my sister's desire to want the best for everyone, because it sure had stolen mine. She was right. Dave was a nice guy, a total catch to some. He wanted to marry me and had said nothing about a prenup. But that didn't change thatt I wasn't completely happy. In my mind, I was okay with being his first wife. Once he got big as a lawyer, he would find him a white woman and leave me. By then, I would have had a child by him that would guarantee me a check and be taken care of no matter what.

The look on my face and my silence must have gotten Brandy's attention. She looked over at me and asked. "What's wrong with you?" "Besides that, you are defending Dave like he's your brother and I'm not your sister," I said to her as I kept looking forward. "No, like seriously, Amber. What is wrong with you? Who hurt you?" she said. "Ain't nothing wrong with me. What are you talking about?" I said back to her. "Mommy must be turning over in her grave. You know damn well she didn't raise us like this. Where did you get these gold digger ways?" she said to me. I gave her a side-eye. "we both know your mother ain't losing no rest over shit that has to do with me. She raised you. She showed me how to fucking survive, no matter what. I didn't get the same love you got. I didn't have the smarts like you. But what I do have, I make work to my benefit." I replied. "What's crazy is you're one of the most intelligent people I know, Amber. I've watched you talk men into risking it all just to give you whatever you want without sleeping with them. If you applied the same skills to a business, you would be excellent and wouldn't need a man for shit, instead of using men and possibly hurting a good one.

Before the conversation could go any more left and possibly ruin my night, I pulled up to liquid and parked. "Oh, hell no! I'm not going into that hole in the wall ass club." Brandy said to me. As she turned and looked at me. "It will be fun I promise." I tried to convince her. "No!" Brandy said. "Brandy, please, this is like the one place that I can go where people don't know me and don't know Dave, so I can be myself. I need this. I need to let my hair down." I said to her with the puppy dog look. Brandy ignored me like I wasn't even talking to her.

I sat there for a moment, then reached into my purse and pulled out my new debit card. Dave added me on the accounts, so I'm buying all our drinks and dinner from wherever you want at the end of the night. After a few moments of silence, she finally said, "fine but I want waffle house and I'm getting whatever I want on the menu" I laughed and nodded my head. We checked over ourselves one more time, and then we got out of the car and proceeded to the line.

As we stood in the back of the line, I impatiently looked over all the females in front of us. There was no way I was waiting in line. These bitches in this line weren't even close to as cute and fine as I and brandy were. So I was about to do what I do best.

I stepped out of line and began walking to the front. I heard Brandy calling my name from behind me; I waved my hand for her to follow me. She looked around nervously first before she finally stepped out of line and followed me. After a few minutes of flirting with the security guard at the door and giving him my number, we were inside.

The club was jumping. There were people everywhere. I swear the hood clubs were where you found some of the finest men and some of the most broke down bitches. Brandy and I made our way to the bar. We found a spot and waited for a bartender. I pulled out my phone to check it when I was bumped. "yo my bad shorty." I heard this man say, and I looked up from my phone to see this light skin man that was fine as hell. He gave you this pretty boy look, but the scar he had going through his eyebrow let me know he had been through some shit. I smiled at him. "It's no problem." I said to him, Brandy nudged me. And I looked over at her and rolled my eyes. Clearly, she would not let me be great tonight. The guy walked off with his drink just as the bartender came over to take our order. I could help but watch as he made his way through the club.

Once the bartender walked away to make our order, Brandy looked at me. "Remember, don't start your shit tonight." She said to me; I waved her off, and I watched ol boy go post up near the dance floor by himself.

Once we had our drink, I led Brandy to the dance floor. We danced together for a while like it was no one but us on the floor. We were just laughing and playing around, having a good old time. The DJ slowed down the vibe and played. Nobody has to know by Kranium. I slowly begin to whine my hips to the beat as I dance all by myself. But before the song could get to the chorus, I felt someone wrap their hands around my hips and ease up behind me. In between me keeping an eye on ol boy. I looked back, expecting it to be ol boy. But instead, it was a dark skin guy with dreads that looked like they had never been touched and a mouth full of gold.

I politely slid his hand down and told him I was good. But no must not have been an answer he was used to because his response was, "bitch its just a dance." As he tried to grab on me. "She said no." Brandy said to him, jumping in. "Mind your business, bitch." He said. "Yo, watch your fucking mouth and take your ass on." I told him, pissed off because now a scene was being made. "It's always you bitches that ain't even that pretty that want to come and shake y'all ass and then get mad when a nigga wants to ease up on you." He said. "Call us a bitch again." Brandy said with her jaw tight.

"Yo, is there a problem here?" ol boy said, stepping in the middle of us. "This ya bitch, Ric?" he asked. "Does it matter?" ol boy said back. "If it ain't ya bitch, this ain't ya issue." He said back to him. "Listen, the lady said she was good on the dance. Take ya horny ass somewhere and go beat ya dick." He said. "Nigga, nobody is scared of you. You out now you want to defend bitches and shit don't get ya self into some shit." The dark skin guy told him as he lifted his shirt, showing his gun.

Brandy looked over at me. And I knew exactly what she was thinking. This was exactly why she didn't want to come in here. "Are you sure this is what you want to do?" ol boy said as he lifted his shirt, revealing his gun too. Just as the dark skin guy was getting ready to say something, his hand moved towards his gun, and ol boy hit him with a two-piece, making him stumble.

From there, the club cleared out because the dark skin guy started letting off shots. I grabbed Brandy's hand and took off running as fast as we could in our heels and didn't stop until we got to the car. "See, this is exactly why I didn't want to go in there." Brandy yelled. "That wasn't my fault." I said to her as we stood at the car and I looked for my keys. "It's not about fault, Amber. Bullets don't have names on them." Brandy said.

Just as I found my keys in my purse, I got a tap on the shoulder. "Excuse me," he said, and I spun around with my fist balled up. "Relax, killer, I just wanted to make sure you were good." He told me I looked ol boy over, and he looked even better outside the club. "Yes, I'm fine. Thanks for asking. I said, blushing. "Amber, let's go." Brandy said. I hit my key fob and unlocked the car doors. "Get in, Brandy," I said to her; I heard her suck her teeth, and then the car door slam.

"So your name is Amber?" he asked. "Yes." I told him. "Rico," he said, extending a hand. "Well, thank you Rico for sticking up for me there." I told him. "No problem. These niggas see a pretty girl and think they going to handle them any type of way and when they are told no, then they want to show out. I hate that shit." He said. "Right." I agreed with him. "Well, can I give you my number? Maybe you can let me know you made it home safe." He said to me, I reached into my purse and pulled out my phone. I looked at the picture of Dave and me on my lock screen before I unlocked the phone and handed it over to Rico to put his number in.

He handed it back to me, and I made sure it was saved. "I'll make sure to hit you." I told him. "You do that," he said as he reached around me and opened my car door. I got in, and he closed the door. He stood there and looked at me and licked his lips as I turned the car on and backed out of my parking spot. "So to the waffle house we go?" I asked, turning my attention to Brandy. "hell no, take me home!" she said. I was in no mood to argue with Brandy or force her to let me spend money on her, so I moved quickly to drop her off so I could hit up Rico.

RICO

I DIDN'T DOUBT NOT one bit that those bullets were meant for me and sent by Chase. But it's something about watching your child being wheeled in on an ambulance stretcher that makes your heart feel like it was outside your chest. I turned Chase in for my family, and now my son had taken a bullet that was for me. As we rushed into the emergency, the nurses stopped Toni and me as other staff rushed my boy to the back.

A nurse handed Toni a clipboard and asked her to fill out some paperwork to get him thoroughly checked in. And once they knew something, they would come to tell us. I grabbed Toni's hand, which was covered with blood, and walked her over to the chairs. She sat down with a blank look on her face, and her legs were shaking. I took a seat next to her and tried to comfort her by rubbing her back. She buried her head in my chest for a few moments. "It's going to be okay, he's a soldier." I said to her, Her head raised, and she looked at me in the eyes. "He's not a soldier. He's a damn child that shouldn't have any memory of his house being shot up two time in a damn row Rico nor a memory of him being shot for that make matter. All cause his daddy to damn weak and useless to fucking protect him!"

"Toni," I said in a voice that revealed all my hurt. "Shut up talking to me. You are the worse fucking thing that ever happened to my kids and me." she said, "but this shit is not even my fault." I said. "It is your fault, Rico, it's all your fault, and when my son pulls through this, my kids and I are out. We want nothing to do with you." She said, "So that's it, you're going to leave me like everyone else." I asked her. "No, Rico, I'm caring about myself and my kids cause all you care about is your damn self!" She told me. "Toni," I said, trying to grab her. "Don't touch me. Leave!" She told me,

I looked at her, confused. "What?" "Get up and leave! You cause more harm when you're here than when you're gone; so leave!" she said. "That's my son!" I told her. "Leave," she yelled. A nurse came over and softly said, "sir at this time can I ask you to leave just for the peace of this woman and the other people waiting here in the waiting room." I looked at her, and then I looked at Toni.

I got up and walked outside. When I got outside, I was pacing back and forth. I pulled my phone out and did something I hadn't done since I had got locked up. I dialed a familiar number. "The number you are trying to reach has been disconnected or changed." I looked at the phone. Dave had the same number since we were kids, and now his number was different. I dailed another number, and when it rang, I felt some relief. "Yo, who is this?" Jayden's voice came through. "Jay, is it Rico?" I said. "Rico?" he asked. "What other Rico do you know?" I asked him. "Why are you calling me?" he asked, and I instantly realized that he was still harboring feelings towards me. "Listen, I really need you and Dave right now." Jayden laughed. "nigga, now you need us, but when we were trying to be there for you. You shut us out all because we wouldn't agree with the shit you wanted to keep doing." I said, "you know what nigga fuck you I only called because my little man in the hospital." I told him. "The fuck you mean your little man in the hospital." Jayden's voice went from somewhat annoyed to complete shock.

"Honestly, Jayden, I fucked up. I should have listened when you niggas told me to get out, but I didn't, and then I got caught up in that case, and jail got crazy. I felt alone; my mom was sick with no one out here to look out for her, so when the fed came to see me and talk about Chase, I did what I thought was best. But them pigs talked like bitches, and Chase know first he sent people to my house the other night tell me to come up with $50,000 and then today my house got hit by a drive-by and my little man got hit." I said, talking fast. "Yo bro, relax... Damn hun. How can I help? What are they saying about little man?" Jayden asked. "Man, I don't even know. Toni doesn't want me up here at the hospital, and she is talking about taking my kids away. Bro, I feel like I failed as a man. I snitched, and I didn't keep my family safe." I said to him as tears streamed down my face.

"Bro relax, let me come get you. We can talk everything out and figure something out. I'm sure between what I got in my Stash, Dave and you; we can come up with something." It wasn't until Jayden said the words Stash that I got a thought in my head. "Nah, you don't have to come get me, bro. I am going to get an uber and go to my mom's house. I told him. 'You sure?" he asked. "Yeah, I'll hit you back later." I told him quickly to hang up and then order an Uber.

The uber pulled up in no time, and I hopped in. I sat in the backseat with my eyes closed and put my head back. And flashed back to my time in jail.

Life was so fucked up that out of all the jails they could have sent me to, I ended up in the same prison as the 16-year-old girl's dad. Being in there alone had me on edge at all times. I always felt like I was being watched, and I was utterly alone. But I tried everything in my ability not to let my mind drive me crazy. This place did enough fucking with your head as it was, and I was determined not to let it win. But I stayed on guard and ready for whatever.

I was in the bathhouse when I felt an arm wrap around my throat and a pointy object on my back. As my eyes watered from the pain, a young dude that I had an issue with when I first got here appeared in front of me with a jail-made knife. There were still marks from the first time we fought on his face. I had beaten him worse than I thought I had. "I'll kill you right now; all the guards are off doing their own thing and we both know they don't give a damn about pedophile ass niggas like you that get caught with little girls that look like their daughters. There's no one here but you, me, and my boys. But that shit would have me in here doing life, and someone thinks you are worth more alive and suffering than dead." he said to me. As he said those words, I saw a figure in the corner of my eyes, and I turned and looked to see Chris, the girl's father, standing there.

The young dude looked over at him, and Chris nodded his head. "I never lose a battle and let it go. I can not kill you right now, but I was paid to make sure you can die slowly and that it's painful for your kids. And as you die mutha fucker, I hope you remember me every bit of the way." he said.

"Nigga, I ain't scared of death! If you bad kill me, clearly that cracker is too scared to do it. So he sent a slave ass nigga like you and ya boy to do it for him," I said, refusing to go down as weak.

The young boy said nothing, but he smiled. And nodded to the big dude that was holding me. I felt movement behind me, and I tried to struggle to free myself. But pain shot through my body as I felt someone ripping me open from behind, the pain went from my ass all the way up to my back. My body went numb, and when the guy that was holding me was done with me, he let me go, and I dropped to the shower floor.

I laid there bleeding out from a stab womb and barely able to breathe. All I wanted to do was die. When I could finally pull myself together, I got up and went to my cell. I never forgot how I felt knowing that I was done in such a way. I never intended to hurt Chris's daughter. And it wasn't my fault her ass would do anything for drugs. I had daughters myself, and I would do anything to protect them, so Although I disagreed, I understood why this happened to me. I sat in my cell silent and did my best to nurse myself. I couldn't tell anyone that, as a grown-ass man, I was raped. All I could do was crawl into my bed and cry in silence.

For weeks, I wouldn't leave my cell. I wouldn't eat, and drinking the water that came out of the sink was the most that I gave myself. I was sure Chris and his people knew what happened to me and were sharing it with everyone. It wasn't until a month and a half later that I stood in my cell with my legs feeling like jello, and then I passed out.

When I came to, I was in the medical area, and I was being asked questions. When did I get stabbed? Why wasn't it reported? Who stabbed me and who I was sleeping with to get HIV. When the C.O. said HIV, I knew he was talking to the wrong person, but he repeated it. "No, you tested positive for HIV and an infection from the stabbing. My heart hit my feet, and what the young nigga said to me finally made sense. He and Chris were going to make sure I died slowly.

JAYDEN

I WAS HIDING out in my office at the barbershop after I visited with Chase. My mind was racing, and I just needed some time to regroup.

I had to figure out how to fix everything. But when Rico hit my line about his son, that fucked me up. A kid getting shot was taking it way too damn far. And I prayed that the little man pulled through. At this point, I am weighing the option of paying Chase off my damn self and then moving Rico out of town, giving him a fresh start. It would just be one of the many secrets that I would have.

As I sat there with my head in my hands, leaning on my desk. There was a knock at my office door, and then it opened. "Yo, whatever it is, it can wait. I don't want to see anybody right now." I said, not even bothering to look up to see who it was. "You don't even want to see me?" Tracey asked? I picked my head up and looked at her. She was smiling at me while she held a to-go food tray in her hands and was dressed in her momma's kitchen shirt, some black leggings, and cros.

"What are you doing here?" I asked her. "Well the restaurant was a little slow, and you never stopped by, so I figured I'd take a brief break and come over here and bring you something to eat." She said to me as she passed me the tray. I opened it, and the smell of the smothered chicken, rice, greens, yams, and cornbread filled my nose and made my mouth water.

Tracey walked around my desk and leaned against it as she looked at me with lustful eyes. "You can fill your stomach with some good food and I can empty your nuts for you." She said, smiling and licking her lips. With all the stress I was under, some head from Tracey would have been great; it was crazy what that mouth of hers could do. It was one of the reasons I was still with her other than our sons we had together. But I quickly remember that after Brandy and I had fucked, I didn't take another shower. Tracey would definitely smell another woman's juices on me.

"As well as that sound bae, I am going to have to pass right now. But I will take you up on that offer later." I told her. "What's wrong with you?" she asked, looking at me confused. "Nothing," I told her quickly. "Jayden, don't lie to me. Because you don't turn down head from me, so something has to be wrong. Ever since Chase went to jail, you were moving differently." She told me. "It's nothing Tracey," I said, becoming annoyed. "mmhm Jayden, I see your ass back lying to me," she said. "Girl, ain't nobody lying to you. Don't start your shit today." I told her.

Me and Tracey's relationship was hard to understand. to everyone on the outside we were the prefect couple. But in reality Tracey was a one night stand that I fucked when I was way to drunk and I got her pregnant. To this day I still think she drugged me. Because back then I was into the club scene heavy and I could throw back a whole bottle of Remy by myself and be fine. But this night Tracey was the bottle girl and brought my bottle over to me and I only got through 75% of the bottle before I was fucked up. I ended up taking Tracey home and fucking her.

We were cool after that but not having sex. then two month later she called and told me she was pregnant. I did nothing for her or the baby until my son was here and I got a D.N.A test. When I knew he was mine and I did what I had to do and moved him and tracey into my house so I could give my son what I didn't have growing up. I was never in love with Tracey but after two kids I learned to love her.

"So if you are not lying to me. Where did you go when you left the house at two o'clock this morning? You were with some bitch, weren't you," she asked, crossing her arms.

Stupid must have been written all over my face because I didn't even know Tracey knew what time I left the house. "Yeah, silence. Go ahead and think of a good lie." She said to me, "Man, I had moves to make." I told her. "What moves does a businessman have to make at those hours, Jayden? You're not in the game any more so it doesn't makes sense." She said, getting loud. "Tracey, chill the fuck out before you make me mad." I told her. "And what you going to do, Jayden, hit me again. Believe me, I ain't scared or worried. All your ass is going to do is apologize after and tell me you'll never do it again." She said, "and all your ass is going to do is stay because without me you're nothing and you know better than to take my sons away from me." I said to her loudly.

"Fuck you, Jayden," she yelled. "Get the hell out with the bull shit Tracey. Take your ass back to the restaurant and go run my business." I demanded. "Fuck you, Jayden, go run your own shit. I'm going to go get my kids and go home." She said, walking out of my office and slamming the door behind her. I shook my head. This was not the time for Tracey to be adding extra stress on me. I needed some stress relief now.

I picked up my phone and dialed Brandy's number. The

phone rang repeatedly, Until it finally went to her voicemail. You've reached Brandy unfortunately I cannot come to the phone. Please leave your name and number, and I'll get back to you. I hung up and took a few bites of my food before finally deciding to just pull up on Brandy. I was sure Brandy was home and studying.

I slapped everyone up as I left the shop, and then I jumped in my car and headed to Brandy's house. When I pulled up, there was a crowd outside, and it looked like there were two bitched out there fighting. I got out of the car and walked up to the crowd. I jumped in quickly when I realized that it was Brandy and Chase's wife Precious fighting. "yo what the fuck are y'all doing?" I said, breaking them apart. "This bitch came to my house on some bullshit." Brandy said. "fuck you bitch, you was fucking my nigga, you dirty ass hoe." Precious yelled as she spits some blood out of her mouth.

Brandy had beaten her ass good. "Bitch, don't be mad at me because your nigga wanted me. Call me another bitch and I'm a fuck you up some more." Brandy responded. "yo y'all buggin out. out here making a scene for these damn people. I told them both. "I don't give a fuck about these people. But I do care about my self-respect." Brandy said. "Fuck that bitch. You are sleeping with someone else, man; you don't get no damn self-respect. And you and Chase bat shit crazy if y'all think I am about to cut a check for this side bitch to get her education." Precious said. "bitch fuck you," Brandy said to her. "Yo Precious go home. I will handle this." I told her. "You better because if I handle it, I am going to fuck her up." Preicous said. "bitch you ain't fuck me up this time." Brandy said, and I wanted to laugh because she was right. "Bitch, you heard what I said, Precious said as she walked away.

I looked at Brandy up and down. "You going to handle me?' she asked with her hands on her hips. "Man, turn that attitude down, and let's go in the house." I told her. "Nah, you can handle me right out here." Brandy said. "Brandy, get in the house now," I yelled, and her eyes got big as she stood there for a few moments and then stomped off.

We got into her apartment, and she went straight to the kitchen. She poured a shot of Remy and threw it back. "Yo, you're too smart to be out here doing this hoodrat shit." I told her. "Yeah, yeah, yeah," she said back to me. "I am serious," I told her. "It doesn't matter how smart I am, that bitch holds the key to my education and I am fucked." Brandy said, and I saw tears start to form in her eyes. I took out my wallet and pulled a debit card from it. "Here, use this to pay for school." I said, slapping the card on the counter. "What about your girl? I don't need another bitch at my doorstep with the fuck shit." She told me. "This is a private account she knows nothing about, so you are good." I told her.

Brandy ran into my arms and hugged me. "Thank you so much, Jayden. I will pay you back, I promise." She told me. "Don't worry about it. I got you and that's all you need to know and focus on." I said. Brandy smiled and then kissed me. When we separated, she took my hand and led me back to her room, and closed the door behind us.

DAVE

"CONGRATULATIONS DAVE, you really deserve this promotion," my boss said to me as he shook my hand. My day had gone from bad to excellent. I finally reached my goal to become the first black lawyer in this firm to make a partner. I couldn't wait to tell Amber and my momma.

I got back to my office and noticed that my mom had been blowing up my phone. I grabbed my stuff and headed out to see her face to face instead of calling her back.

It took me no time to get to my momma's house, and I got out of the car with a pep in my step and a smile on my face. I let myself in the house, and my momma was sitting on the couch angrily. "So you ain't see me calling you?" She said with her Puerto Rican accent coming out, letting me know she was mad. "I was in a very important meeting mom but I'm here now." I told her. "What could have been more important than answering me." She asked. "I made partner at the firm." I said to her, smiling.

She smiled and hugged me. "Baby, I am so proud of you. I know how hard you worked for this. Your daddy would be so proud." She said to me, "Yes, everything is falling right in place.

I made partner; now I really feel comfortable marrying Amber." I said, and I watched the smile quickly fade from my mommas.

"What's wrong momma?" I asked her, looking concerned. "Son, something just doesn't feel right to me about that girl." She said, "Momma, I keep telling you I love Amber. She is the best thing that ever happens to me. She makes me a better man. She taught me how to love someone other than you, despite how scary it is. She helped me see that life is better with someone to share it with. And that there is no amount of money more important than the smile on someone else's face. Momma, I just want what you and daddy had." I told her.

"David, in order for you to have what me and your dad had, the love has to actually be real!" She responded. "Momma it is. I promise you." I told her. "David, I'm telling you Amber is a gold digger and she's going to hurt you badly especially if you marry her. Be careful, baby. Cause no matter how old you are, you are still my baby and I will go to hell and back for you." I smiled at her words. I know, momma. "You really don't, baby. But I would hate to have to show that other side of me." She said,

"Okay mom. Well, I have something else to tell you. take a seat" I said thinking that there was no better time then now to get this shit out there, "what's that?" She asked. "Ricos home." My mom's face lit up. "Where is he? When did you pick him up? What time is he coming over? I got to cook him a good meal." She spits out. "I don't know." I told her. "You don't know what, David?" Her mothering voice set in. "I don't know where he is momma. He's been out for almost 6 months now and I only found out because his name came up in a case I'm working."

"I knew this would happen," she said. "What?" I asked. "That sister of mine would run him off. Her cold hearted ass fucked him up so bad that he didn't even come home." She said, "Momma, I don't think it's like that." I said. "How would you know David? You don't know my sister." She blurted out as she paced back and forth. "I know, because Rico has been in touch with Auntie Clara. And I know that because I've been taking care of Auntie Clara." "You've been doing what?" She asked. "She has breast cancer, momma. And Rico has H.I.V," I told her. My mom took a seat on the couch with her mouth open. "I got to go see her. I have to comfort her." She said with tears forming in her eyes. "Momma, don't go to Auntie Clara's house." I said. "Lil' boy, who are you to tell me where to go and where to not go?" She asked me. "Momma, I already been trying to work you back into auntie Clara's life. She is not trying to have it and if you go over there, she will shut me out too."

The room was silent, and I watched the same hurt show up on my mom's face that was there the day my dad died. I sat on the couch next to my mom and let her cry into my chest. "Momma, it's going to be okay." I told her. With her eyes puffy and nose red, she looked at me. "Find him. Bring my other baby home to me." She told me.

RICO

IT TOOK my uber driver no time to get to my mother's house. When he pulled up, I sat and looked at the home for a while; it always seemed like there was a gray cloud over this house. It had been so long since I had been here, and although I loved my mother when I got released from jail, I couldn't bring myself to come to see my mother at her lowest point. When it came to her, I was still like a little kid, and I wanted nothing more but for her to love me. But once I started making money and selling drugs, all she cared about was what I could do for her. Jayden and Dave hid what we did from Auntie Dorothie; on the other hand, I was honest with my mom and even supplied her from time to time.

My mom's addiction never let her love on me the way Aunt Dorothie loved on me, and Dave. As a matter of fact, I never recall her saying she loved me. Cancer and me being in jail had softened her, but never changed her completely.

I got out and went to the door. I hesitated before I knocked. "Fuck it, I'm here for my son." I said to myself. I hit, and I could hear someone moving around. It was a few moments before the door opened, and my mom flew into my chest and cried. "Your home. My baby is home." She cried. I wrapped my arms around her and hugged her. She was always skinny before, but now it was like she was nothing in my arms and even this hug made me feel like I was going to break her.

"baby I've missed you so much, come in." She said to me, taking my hand. I came into the house, and everything was still the same as it was when I was a kid. "So, did you bring me something?" she asked as she took a seat on the couch. "Bring you what?" I asked her. "You know that good stuff." she said. "Mom, you have cancer. You don't need to be putting that shit in your body on top of whatever they are already pumping in you to keep you alive." I told her as I stormed off to my old bedroom.

I walked into the room, and everything was still the same. I could hear my mom slowly making her way down to where I was. I moved the bed and lifted a floorboard. "Rico, what are you in there doing? Dont be tiring up my house. And if you don't have what I need, don't be getting comfortable here." She said, sounding winded.

I pulled the box from under the floorboard that I had been stashing money in for years when I was out. I consider it my rainy day fund, and with the time I was locked up, I had forgotten all about it until today. As I opened the box and the money fell out. My mom appeared in the doorway. "Where did that money come from?" she asked. I said nothing; I just began to count, hoping that I had enough. "Remario Peris, do you not hear me talking to you?" she yelled.

"Mom, I have been stashing money here for years just in case anything ever went wrong." I said to her, "Just in case anything went wrong? Remario, what do you call this? I have cancer. This place is falling apart and I barely have enough money to handle my medicine, let alone my bills." She said as I kept counting. "Boy, keep ignoring me and I am going to..."

"going to what Momma hit me. Well, guess what? I'm not some little ass boy scared of you no more. And you're not the woman you used to be. I'm a grown ass man and you're not getting this money or any money from me. I have to save my son and family." I said to her,

"Rico, what the hell are you talking about?" she said. "Fuck," I yelled when I realized I only had $20,000 stashed away. I sat there thinking. Then I went to my closet and found a bag and tossed the money in there. "Rico?" My mom yelled. And I looked up at her with tears in my eyes. "I have to take this money and divide it up and you need to pack. When Remario jr gets out of the hospital Toni needs to take her and the kids and move. I have to move you, Bianca and Monique." I told her. "What is going on? I've never seen you this worked up before." She said, "Mom, I am in real deep with Chase. He had my house shot up and little Remario got shot. Now I have to do what I have to do to fix this." I told her as I got all the money in the bag and headed out of the room.

"Rico, I'm not moving anywhere. My doctors are here. My house is here. No little boy is going to run me out of this town. You handle this shit. And you handle it NOW and I want an update on my grandson as soon as you get one." she demanded, following me back to the living room. "Clara, this shit is not up for decision. Take this money pack, you shit, and be ready." I told her, slamming some money on the coffee talk as my eye got stuck on an invitation. I picked it up and read it. You are invited to the wedding of Amber and David. It said with a picture of the same Amber I was just dicking down in a hotel room and my cousin.

"What the hell is this?" I said to my mom. "Dave is getting married. You would have known if you would just speak to the boy. He is doing great for himself. He paid off his momma house, got a place out his the suburbs, he and that girl drive fancy cars and he been paying the bills around here. He's doing so good that she doesn't even work." My mom told me. I looked at her because she didn't even realize she had just told on herself about the bill not being paid. But that was the least of my worries. As she spoke, a thought came to mind. "Mom, I got to go, but stay by your phone. Okay?" I said, as a second idea came to mind.

Amber

AS I DROVE HOME, my phone rang. I looked, and it was Rico. "hey zaddy." I cheerfully said when I answered the phone. "Where are you?" he barked into the phone. "On my way home." I told him. "Bring your ass over now!" Rico commanded. "But Rico, I have to.." Rico interrupted me, "I didn't ask you what you had to do. Get here now!" Rico said, and then hung up.

I busted a U-turn and headed to Rico's and I's usual meeting spot. All that was getting my shit together, talk had gone out the window just that damn quick. I pulled up to the park Rico, and I usually met at, and shortly after I parked my car, I saw Rico's car pulling up behind me quickly. He jumped out of his car and came and got into mine.

"Hey baby," I said to him as I leaned over to hug him and kiss. "Fuck all that nice shit," he said as he mushed me. "I need 50 stacks and I need it in 48 hours. "Rico was normally a little aggressive in how he talked, but never like this. "Rico, I don't have $50,000. where am I supposed to get that type of money for you, baby?" I said to Rico.

Rico pulled out his gun and sat it on his lap. I looked, and for the first time, I feared Rico. "bitch stop playing with me. Get the Fuckin money from Dave." I looked at him with my eyes wide, "How do you know about Dave?" at the sound of Rico speaking Dave's name like he was someone we talked about on the regular.

Rico laughed, but this wasn't his usual laugh. This laugh was evil. "He's my cousin, stupid. My mom showed me y'all wedding invites that came in the mail the other day. So, imagine my thoughts when I see the bitch I'm fucking and my cousin's engagement pictures." I cried. "Rico, listen, I wasn't trying to play you, I swear." "Bitch, you couldn't play me even if I let you. Bitch, you are nothing." he said to me. "Why are you doing this, do the last six months we spent together mean nothing to you." Rico busted out laughing. "AWW hoe you thought I loved you? Man, go get my money from Dave or I'll kill you and him. But not before I tell him I was fucking his fiance for the last six months and his bitch has swolled my kids several times and soaked in my nuts and then came home to him and probably kissed his ass without brushing her teeth."

My heart was in my feet at this point. "Rico, I can't just get 50 stacks out of him, maybe 1 or 2. But any more than that and he's going to want to know what the money's for." I cried out to him. Rico looked at me with a rage in his eyes. "Bitch, that ain't my problem. Tell him it's for that fucking wedding. Or shit tell him the truth, it's keeping a bullet out of both of yall asses." Rico said, as he got out of my car and slammed my door behind him.

I drove home shaking. I didn't know what to do or how the hell I would get $50,000 out of Dave to give to Rico. But my mind was going a thousand miles per hour, trying to figure out how I would save my ass. When I pulled up in our driveway, I didn't see Dave's car. I sat in the car for a while and wiped my face while I thought. Then I came up with an idea I would take all the expensive jewelry Dave got me and some of his, and I'd pawn it. Then I would buy all the jewelry back one by one as I got the money before Dave realized anything was missing. As long as I didn't pawn my engagement ring, he wouldn't notice. I told myself.

I went into the house and grabbed a duffle bag. I quickly put as much stuff as possible that I thought would equal up to $50,000 in the bag. When I heard Dave's car in the driveway, I stuffed the bag under our bed and rushed to meet him at the door.

I greeted him the way I always did, cheerfully and with a kiss while trying to do my best to hide how I was feeling. "Hey baby, how was your day?" I asked. "It was great. You are looking at the new partner at the firm," Dave said proudly. I jumped up and down, rejoicing. "Baby girl, go get dressed, we are going out to celebrate." he told me.

I went to our bedroom, pulled out a sexy black dress, and laid it on the bed. Then my phone rang. Dave walked in the room taking off his work clothes, and I told him he could jump in the shower first, that it was Brandy, and I wanted to talk to her a little. Dave said, okay. By that time, my phone had stopped ringing. By the time Dave grabbed his towel and walked to the bathroom, it was ringing again. I waited until I heard Dave close the bathroom door and the shower water come on before answering my phone. "Hello," I said. "Bitch, you got my money yet?" Rico yelled into the phone. "No, not yet. I'm getting it though." I answered by sounding nervous. Rico said nothing and hung up.

Dave came out of the bathroom, and I went in. I showered and come out. When I walked into the room, I saw the bag of jewelry on the bed, and Dave was looking at me. "Amber, what's this?" he asked. "Huh?" I said while I stood there wrapped in a towel, looking stupid. I was thinking of what to say, but my mind had gone completely blank. "If you can, huh? You can hear. Why is all our jewelry in this bag?" he asked. "I don't know." I said to him, Dave looked at me. "So my cufflink rolled under the bed and I went to get it and found this. And you telling me you don't know how this duffle bag full of our jewelry got under our bed? Amber stopped playing with me. Clearly it wasn't a robbery because robbers normally take shit like this with them." Dave said.

I didn't know what to say, so I burst into tears. Dave looked at me, confused, and walked over to hold me. "Amber, please tell me what's going on. Whatever it is, we can work it out." I looked at Dave and said, "can we work through anything?' Dave wiped my tears with his thumb, "of course I love you." he told me. "You might want to have a seat." I said to him,

He sat on the edge of the bed and pulled me onto his lap. I poured out everything. When I was done, he sat there in silence for a while. Then he pushed me off of him, stood up, and grabbed his wallet and his keys off the dresser. "Baby, where are you going?" I asked him. "I'm going to pay this dummy the $50,000 he's asking for. Because he is that stupid to kill me and you over a quick dollar. This Mutha fucker doesn't have shit to lose at this point. He's been to jail. That shit doesn't bother him And I love you too much to let that happen."

I smiled and walked over to my Superman to kiss him. But Dave pushed me back and said: "you need to pack." I looked at him, confused. "Huh?" I told him. "Pack your stuff, Amber," he shouted. I cried again. "I thought you said we can work through this." Dave looked at me and shook his head as he said, "the cheating I could have worked through. But with him...." I interrupted him, "because he's your cousin." I spoke with my head down. "Nah, because he's HIV positive and I don't like my life being at risk."

Brandy

MY PHONE RANG, waking me from my sleep. I rolled over in bed and picked it up off the nightstand. "Hello," I answered as I put the phone to my ear with my eyes still closed. "Brandy," I heard Amber say like she was crying. "Yeah," I responded. She said nothing, but I could hear her crying. "What's going on Amber?" I asked. I sounded annoyed.

He found out." she cried out into the phone. "What?" I asked her, sitting up in bed and giving her my full attention. "Dave found out about Rico." she said. A devilish smile came over me, and I did everything I could not to laugh. But I had only been telling Amber that this love triangle of hers would end badly since she met Rico one night we were in the club.

"What do you mean? What happened? Are you okay?" I asked her, trying to sound genuine and sympathetic, like I cared. "No, I'm not okay. Shit is falling apart brandy." She said, In my head, all I could think about was how the mighty had fallen.

I got up from the bed and grabbed my robe to cover my naked body. I looked over at Jayden's fine dark skin ass, sleeping so peacefully after I had put all this good pussy on him. I walked out into my living room and took a seat. "Okay, tell me what's going on sissy." I told her.

"so my day was going well, then I went to this stupid ass women's empowerment meeting, and it was super inspiring I had my head on straight and was ready to walk away from Rico. Then, on my way home, Rico called me. I went to meet up with him and this nigga gets in my damn car and demands I give him $50,000." She tells me.

"That's crazy," I told her, so she knew I was listening. "I told him I don't have $50,000 just lying around to give him, and he told me to get it from Dave. "Wow, how did he know about Dave?" I asked her. "So here's the crazy part: they are fucking cousins, Brandy." she said. "Who?" I asked her. "Rico and Dave. they are cousins," she told me. "I know you fucking lying," I said to her.

"That's not even that icing on the damn cake. I was so scared because Rico was threatening to kill me and Dave if he didn't get the $50,000 that I came home and bagged up our jewelry," she said to me. "Amber, what the hell were you going to do with the jewelry?" I asked her. "So I came up with the idea to pawn it; to get the money for Rico so no one would get hurt." she explained.

"wouldn't it have just been easier to just go to the bank and get the money?" I asked her. "Don't you think if it was that easy I would have just done that Brandy. Damn. But taking $50,000 out is not a small unnoticeable amount." She said, "But taking jewelry?" I asked her, rolling my eyes. "I was just trying to figure everything out. Plus, Dave's mom had him put all the accounts back in his name only. "She explained, and I couldn't help but think how stupid my sister was. "So you mean to tell me all this time y'all been together and you are about to marry this man and he is still listening to his mom over you? Not to mention your name, not on shit?" I asked her.

"All the money is Dave's. He takes good care of me. If it wasn't for this situation, I would not need to access the money because whatever I ask for I get." she told me. "You don't even have a stash of money hidden away somewhere?" I asked her. "No," she answered quickly. It was official. My sister was dumb. Every woman in history had a secret. Stash of money hidden away that her man knew nothing about just in case something happened.

"Damn," I said into the phone. "Damn is right. I got my ass in the shower and the bag of jewelry was under the bed. I came out of the bathroom and Dave had found the bag. At that point, all I could do was come clean. After I told him everything, he stormed out of here like a madman. And told me to get out."

The smile I once had was back and even bigger this time. I did everything I could to hide my happiness in my voice when I said, "sis if you need somewhere to go while Dave cools off you can come here. It's not exactly the suburban living you're used to, but it was something." I told her. " I don't think this is going to just blow over like you think, Brandy." she told me. "Of course it will. Dave is a really nice guy, and he loves you. He's just hurt right now. He's going to cool off and take you back. Just watch." I said, trying to be encouraging even though I hoped Dave left her ass alone.

"Brandy he's passed hurt. I did the unthinkable. I exposed him and myself to H.I.V fucking with Rico." my phone dropped from my hand as I sat there with my mouth wide open, shocked by what Amber had just said.

"Brandy... Brandy..." I heard AMber saying. I picked my phone back up and put it to my ear. "Yes?" I answered. " I don't know what to do." She said to me, ``You need to make a damn appointment to get tested. damn Amber, you fucked that nigga raw. you clearly don't even know him like that and you meet him in the fucking club." I said, hoping she heard all the judgment in my voice.

"it was only once and by mistake. Rico was always so strict about wrapping it up and not letting me give him head, and I used to wonder why cause he never once said he had H.I.V. That one time we got caught up in the moment and he never put the condom on." She said to me. "Bitch, you realize that nigga was trying to fucking kill you, right? H.I.V is not a fucking joke, it's a damn life changing sentence." I told her. "I know I Know I Know. I feel like this is Karma for cheating in the first place. I'm so stuck I don't know what to do." Amber's dumb ass said.

"You need to go to a clinic or doctor's office as soon as they open in the morning." I said. "And then what?" she said, all hopeless. I looked at the phone. "Girl, you know what I got to go. I'll be over in a few, you dropping a way to many damn bombs on me on this phone. " Amber got quiet, I rubbed my head "damn Amber," I said. "I know I didn't expect things to happen like this." she said. I rolled my eyes. What she meant was she didn't expect to get caught. "Umm, give me some time to get dress I'll be over cause this just too fucking much to handle over the phone." I said. "Okay." she responded, and then we hung up.

I put my phone down and shook my head. "She didn't expect it to be like this. I bet she fucking didn't," I said as I laughed. I loved my sister, but I hated her at the same damn time, and this was just another way of showing that she never deserved this lifestyle or Dave. She thought of no one but herself; it was all about Amber, what she wanted and that was it.

I walked into my room and turned on the bright light. "Damn Brandy," Jayden said as he covered his face. "Get up," I said. "What am I getting up for," he said. "Because you got to go. And I am sure that your baby mother is probably looking for you." I said. Jayden rolled over and gave me a look. "I'm not talking about her, I am just saying." I replied.

Jayden pulled me into the bed with him. "You really want me to go home to her? You sure you don't want any more of this?" he asked me as he humped my leg a little. "As good as that sounds, I got to go check on Amber. Shit, just got real." I told him. "What do you mean?" he asked. "Rico and Amber were messing around and he tried to get the $50,000 out of Amber." I told him.

"Fuck!" Jayden said, throwing his hands over his face like he knew more than what I told him. "What?" I asked him. "He's desperate." Jayden said. "who?" I asked, confused. "Rico, Chase had his house shot up. And his son got hit." he said. "Are you serious?" I asked "hell yeah and what he doesn't know is even if he gets the money Chase will not stop." he said with a serious look on his face.

"That's not even all Amber told me; she told me that Rico and Dave are cousins," I said to him. "I know, and Rico has H.I.V," Jayden said to me. I looked at him, confused. "How do you know this?" I asked. "Because Rico, Dave, and I used to be boys, we ran together. Sold drugs for Chase together and even lived together. No one knows that but us." he said to me. "Suddenly, I was trying to figure out what the hell I had gotten myself into.

Amber

AFTER HOURS of crying and talking to Brandy, she got an Uber and headed home. I laid in bed, replaying everything in my head repeatedly until I finally dozed off for a few mintues and when I woke up, today wasn't like any of the other days I had spent with Dave.

I rolled over, and no one was in my king-size bed but me. No one was there to tell me I was beautiful. No one was loving on me. I wasn't sure where we stood. If I was still getting married or what. But I was convinced that I missed Dave, and I was sorry. I picked up my phone and called him. Although, Brandy told me after last night to stop blowing up his phone; he needed his time.

I was thankful that I had my sister to be there for me through this. But she wasn't letting me off easy.

Talking to Brandy really let me know I needed to go be seen as soon as possible, and then I needed to figure out how I was going to fix all this shit. So here I was sitting in the damn clinic. I had been watching the clock since they drew my blood. And I felt like with every tic that the clock made; I was that much closer to; losing it and walking out. This was the longest, most embarrassing twenty minutes of my life.

The door finally opened, and it felt like my heart hit my feet and the wind was knocked out of me. The doctor came in, looking down at the paperwork on her clipboard. "well amber..." she said, leaving a long pause. "Well, what?" I told her with an attitude because this damn sure was not the time for the long dramatic breaks. My life was on the line. Dave's life was on the line. And all I could think of was how I was still torn between the two of these men.

A piece of me wished I never met Rico and that I just stayed loyal to Dave. Another part of me thought that if I had H.I.V., this was a sign that Rico and I were meant to be together because no one else would want me with this disease.

"As of right now, you are H.I.V. free, but I suggest you continue to be tested regularly. And that you have anyone else that you have possibly been sexually active with tested too." She said, and I felt the life coming back to me. "Okay, so can I get that in some type of writing that I am clean so I can get out of here." I asked her as I stood up and got off of the examination bed. "Yes, I can give it to you with your prenatal prescription." the doctor responded. "Pre- what?" I asked her, taking a seat.

"Amber, you're pregnant. Did you not know?" she asked me. "Hell no!" I responded to her. "Well, you are nine weeks along." I sat there silent for a while, then I finally asked. "what if I don't want to keep it?" I asked her. And she looked up at me, confused. "Why wouldn't you want to keep your baby Amber?" she asked. "Because right now my life is not set up for a baby." I answered.

She looked at me with a disapproving look. "Well you are still in your first trimester, so there are options there for you. But I suggest you reach out to your OBGYN to discuss them." She told me, "thank you. Can I leave now? I have other things to handle?" I told her. I nodded my head. I got ready to go. I took my phone out to look, and they're was still no word from Dave.

I went to my car, and I had a text from Rico asking if I had his money yet. I responded no, and he let me know not to play with them. I loved this man, and I couldn't even understand why he was treating me like this. But my heart told me I needed to be ready for whatever price I had to pay for what I had done.

I pulled up in my and Brandy's old hood. This was so beneath me, and I was mad I was even back here. I didn't even come to see Brandy because I didn't want to be reminded of this place. I drove around for a few and then I saw the person I was looking for. I rolled down my window and slowly eased up. The niggas standing with Jason ran off, and Jason was about to hall ass until I said. "Boy, where the hell are you going?" I said.

Jason turned around and laughed. "Man Amber, don't be easing up on the block like that. You know when cars ease up like we think they drive by." he said. "Yeah, yeah, yeah, but I needed them niggas you was with gone. I don't need nobody in my face and nobody telling my sister I was around here." I told him. Jason came and leaned in the car with his blueberry cologne filling my nose. Jason was my childhood neighbor, and he was still as fine as he was when we were young, and I was crushing on him. It was said that he was so smart, a straight-A student at all times. But yet the hood had snatched him up and made him nothing but another hood nigga. "Girl, you're still fine as hell," he said to me.

I smiled. "Thanks, but I need your help." I said to him, "You know I'll do anything for Amber." he said with this funny voice. "I need a piece?" I said. "For what?" he asked me. "Don't worry about it. Just know I need it." I said. Jason looked me in the eye for a while and then said, okay, I got you. Let me get in, and we can go around the corner and get you right." Jason said.

We pulled up to this building, and Jason hopped out quickly and went inside. While he was gone, I sent a text to Dave, and there was still no response. Jason came back quickly. He got in the car and then pulled a small gun from under his shirt. I knew nothing about the names of guns or anything else, so I wasn't sure if this was a good one. But as long as I ever needed it, it let off shots. I was good.

"Here," he said, giving it to me. "Thank you," I said, turning to the back seat to get my purse. Jason put up his hand. "This one on me. Something tells me you really need it." he said. I looked at him. "Thank you," I said again with a feeling of relief because the $400 I had in my purse was all the money I had, I had taken it off my prepared card just for this. but I was going to give it to him for the peace of mind of knowing I can protect myself.

Jason sat in the car with me for a few more mintues and showed me how to work the gun. But that was interrupted when I got a call from Dave. I answered in a quickness. Dave ignore me and what I was saying and told me to inform Rico to meet up with him at their grandma house. my heart started to race. I told Jason I had to go and, I made some moves. While in motion I called Rico to relay the message.

RICO

I WENT BACK to the house and packed some things for Toni and the kids. I looked at all the holes in the walls and replayed the whole situation in my head repeatedly with tears in my eyes. This shit was never supposed to be like this. My family was never supposed to be on the run or hiding because of the shit I did. But I was going to fix it. I was going to send them all off. And stay here and face what was going on. If I died in the mix. I was okay with that as long as they were safe.

I called Bianca and Monique and told them what was going on. After they both cussed me out and I had to remind them who I was. The plan was set. They were going to make moves, and I was going to get them the money. The last person I had to deal with was Toni. and I knew it would be hard with everything that was going on.

I called Toni's phone repeatedly, trying to see if she'd let me come back to the hospital so we could talk face to face and I could at least know if my little man was okay, but there was no answer. But he was not answering. I figure she needs more time.

The morning had come, and I was tired of playing the

games with Toni, and I wanted to know what was going on with my damn son, so I got an uber and headed to the hospital. I arrived back at the hospital first thing in the morning. Toni wasn't sitting out in the waiting room anymore. I walked up to the front desk to get some information from the nurse. "Hello ma'am, I was here yesterday and left. My baby mom was waiting for my son to come out of surgery." I said to her, ''What is your son's name?" she asked as if I was annoying her as she popped her gum and never even looked up from the computer. "Remario Piers Jr." I told her. She went to typing on the computer.' she was silent for a few moments and then finally she said "he's stable." and popped her gum, still never looking up from her computer screen.

    I looked at this woman like she had three heads. "That's it?" I asked. "Yeah, that's it," she responded with an attitude. "Bitch, are you serious?" I asked her. "Excuse me?" she said, finally looking up at me. "You're right. Excuse you because your ass is rude and heartless. Your ass needs a new job if this is how heartless you are about someone's loved ones. That is my fucking son. You just pulled up in the damn system and told me he was stable like he was nothing. I'm sure that when you pulled him up you saw that he was only seven and here cause he was shot. So how fucking dare you treat someone like that. Your simple ass didn't even ask if I'd like to see him or anything. Do you know I will come across this desk and choke the fuck out of you?" I said.

    As I ripped that nurse apart, the same one who asked me to leave yesterday showed up. "Mr. Peris?" she said, coming over to me. "Listen, if you about to try to make me leave again, this time it will not work." I told her. "No, not at all. I want to take you to see your son." she said to me.

    She walked me back to the room, and I stopped when I got to the door. I never wanted to see any of my kids in a situation where they got cords and tubes hanging from them or attached to machines. I felt like I failed as a man, a father, a provider and a protector. The nurse looked at me and grabbed my hand. "He will be okay. Surgery went well. He is in a medicine induced coma just so we can handle and control the pain he's in. But he's a strong little boy. And I'm sure he needs his daddy to be strong as well. You can go in and talk to him. He can still hear you." She said, This was beyond the treatment I was expecting to get from the nurse.

She walked away, and I stepped into the room and saw Toni sleeping on the couch. I went over to the bed and stood over my son and rubbed my hand across his face. "Hey little man. You're one strong little boy. I am so sorry that you got caught up in this shit behind me. You know, being your dad was the best thing I ever did in my life. But the bad I've done caught up to me and affected you. You and your siblings deserve so much more than this shit, and I am going to make sure that happens because I want all of you to be better than me. When you, your momma and sister move, I want you to make sure you take good care of them. Protect them. Be the man that I couldn't be." I said to him with a tear falling down my face.

"Move?" Toni said, making me turn towards her. "Listen, I am not trying to argue with you. I am sorry Toni, and I want to get you and the kids away from all of this. Here, take this bag. Once little man gets out of her call, Bianca, Monique and Momma. all of you need to meet up in Texas. I am depending on y'all to be a family and raise my kids together because they will need y'all and each other." Toni was crying. "Rico, what are you talking about? Where are you going?" she asked me.

Before I could answer her, my phone rang. I took it out and saw a number. I didn't know. "Yo?" I answered and Amber's voice came through. she informed me that David wanted me to meet him at my grandma's house. I wasn't sure what was going on, but if this was God's way of giving me a second chance, I was going to take it.

"Toni, I got to go. But just know I love you. I always have and I always will. I am so sorry for the things I put you through." I said to her as I kissed her and then walked out of the hospital room.

I got another uber and headed to my destination as I rode in the car. I picked up my phone and made one more call.

"Hello?" My momma's voice came through the phone. "Hey mom," I said. "Rico, where are you? And how is the baby?" she said to me. "Momma, Toni is going to be reaching out to you. What she tells you, I just want you to go with no hassle. If anything happens to me, I want you to do for my kids what you didn't do for me and that's love them unconditionally." I said. "Rico, what the hell are you talking about?" she said. As much as I hoped Dave was going to have the money, I also knew that my 72 hours were ending. "Momma, just love them, please. That is all I ask of you and with all the hurt you cause me. And the fact that you weren't the best mother you should have for me, and I don't blame you for that anymore. I feel like that's the least you can do. I love you mom." I said as we approached the house, and I hung up.

DAVE

RING, Ring, Ring

"Yo!" Jayden said when he answered.

"Yo, I need you to take a ride with me'" I said into the phone.

"Aww shit, now what the fuck done happen? You only want me to take a ride with you when it's some crazy shit going on." Jayden said in a joking manner.

"I'll tell you in the car," I said back.

"Alright, my nigga, pull up," Jayden told me.

"I'm already outside," I told him.

When Jayden came outside and got into the car, I pulled off. I could see Jayden looking at me from the concer of my eye, and he looked a little worried. "Nigga, what the fuck is wrong with you. You look crazy right now." Jayden said worriedly. "Man, when the hell did Rico get out of jail," I said and Jayden's eyes got a little bugged out. "Nigga, what Rico you talking about? Jayden said, confused. "My cousin Rico, the one that is supposed to be doing over a five-year bid right now for that selling drugs to a minor charge that I couldn't get him off for," I said to Jayden, almost shouting. "Oh, Rico with the package. Shit, hell if I know, that ain't my man. Why what's up? Why are you worried about him?"

"Man Amber dumb ass has been out here fucking this nigga. Now, this nigga wants 50 stacks from me or he going to Kill me and her. "I said back while looking at Jayden at a red light. "Man, first off, I told you that bitch wasn't shit when you first got with her when she was walking around still wearing 27 pieces as a bartender. Second, that nigga got the package. Have you been fucking that bitch raw? Have you gotten tested? Third fuck him. I know damn well you not about to let this nigga get you for 50 stacks. Not when we got heat for little niggas like him." Jayden said with his chest pumped out and holding his gun he had tucked in the front of his pants.

"Man, I ain't got no choice. That little stupid nigga ain't got shit to live for. He's already dying inside. He'll risk it all and really try to kill me over 50 stacks." I said sadly. "Man, you better man up. Being around them white people done made you soft. The Dave I know that went by Diggy in these streets wouldn't stand for this." Jayden said as he pulled out his gun and tried to hand it to me.

"Man, that was over 10 years ago. I'm not that person any more. I am a lawyer. I defend the murders. I'm not one. I left that hot boy lifestyle alone when I got accepted into law school, you know this man." I said. "Man, just because you a lawyer that makes you the perfect murder because you know what not to do that gets you clients caught. Nigga let just roll out on his ass. I got your back, and you got mine just like the old days. I'm not about to watch you pay this nigga $50,000 for no bitch. Shit, I'll pull the trigger. Fuck it. Nobody is going to miss his ass, anyway." Jayden snarled.

I drove around in my thoughts, toning Jayden out. I was battling with myself about what I knew was right and what I knew was wrong. One-shoulder, I have one monkey sounding like Jayden, and on the other shoulder, I had another monkey telling me I had too much to live for to go back to the person Jayden wanted me to be. Not to mention Jayden had no idea how far Diggy would go. No matter which one I did wouldn't stop the hurt Amber has caused me.

"Yo, Dave, Dave, DIGGY!" Jayden yelled. "What?" I screamed back. "Man, I'm talking to you, and you are zoned out. What are you going to do? Both Amber and Rico deserve to die. They got you all the way fucked up. "We can handle Rico, and I can have my baby mom and her girls run down on Amber's old dirty ass. Jayden said, "Nah, Amber remains untouched no matter what. I still love her. I told Jayden.

"WHAT? My guy, you bugging that bitch put your life in danger in more ways than one because she clearly doesn't love you." Jayden was saying until I yelled and interrupted him. "I know Jayden, I know. But I love her, and that doesn't just go away overnight. And to be honest, I knew she was cheating. I just didn't know with who. I'm not dumb. I knew when the pussy felt different, someone else had been in it. When I got the feeling, I started strapping up. Her slow ass never even asked why I started using condoms again. I also started getting tested every three months. As of right now, I'm clean but I got another check up coming up and I'm scared as hell because I know what this nigga has." I said to Jayden sincerely.

"Man, take me home because you are bullshitting and sounding more and more like a bitch," Jayden said as he picked up his phone. "I'm acting like a bitch because I'm deciding not to get my hands dirty anymore? Busting my gun is not my solution to everything no more. WE AREN'T KIDS ANYMORE MORE JOC." I said to Jayden, almost in tears. "Nah, you a bitch, because you are not handling this shit at all, you are about to cry." Jayden sat back and said nothing else.

I drove Jayden home in silence. Since pre-K, they had been

best friends, so he knew he was just saying what he thought was best for me. It was just that he couldn't see it from my side because our lives were so different. We choos to leave the game at the same time. But he still chooses to be attached to the streets in a way while I decide to go legit. I pulled up to Jayden's house, and before he got out, he turned and looked at me. "Man dog, no matter what you decide, I'm down with you, remember that"

I dropped Jayden off and drove to an empty lot to think. I pulled out my phone. All this time, I was driving around. I never checked my phone after hanging up with Jayden. I had 50 missed calls and 70 text messages. They were all from Amber. When I looked at the message's preview, they all were of her saying the same thing.

Baby, I'm sorry

I didn't mean to hurt you.

Baby, I didn't know it was going to be like this.

I'm so sorry

Would you please call me?

Please forgive me

Come home

We can fix it

I couldn't worry about the shit Amber was saying, and honestly, I didn't want to hear it. But I needed to talk to her. I needed her to contact Rico.

Ring Ring Ring

"Baby, oh my god, are you okay?" Amber said as soon as she answered the phone. "Amber, call Rico and tell him to meet me at Grandma Lisa's house at noon," Dave said to her. "Okay baby, but are you coming home soon?" she asked. "I told you to get out," Dave said, then hung up.

time came and passed. I hadn't gotten any sleep, or even eaten, because my mind was racing. I didn't even go home because I knew Amber was most likely still there. I went to my mom's house, showered and changed clothes, and put on a sweatsuit that had been there since god knows when. Thank god she wasn't home because I didn't have it in me right now to break down any of what was going on to her.

I went to the five different banks and withdrew the money I needed for this meeting. Then I headed to my grandma's house. My grandma passed away some years ago. But I bought her house as a gift to my family to lose something that so many of us had memories of. The house was still the way it was when my grandma was alive, and the fresh flower on the dining room table let me know my mom had been there lately.

Noon rolled around quickly, and I could feel a knot growing in my throat. When the knock at the door came, I had to clear my throat just to say come in. I stood at the head of the dining room table as Rico entered the home.

"Oh, shit, your bougie-ass really here, you came to face me like a man," Rico said, laughing.

"Rico man, come on we don't have to do this man we family." I pleaded with him.

Rico pulled his gun and said, "Fuck family. Family let me sit in jail for over 2 and a half years. Now give me my fuckn money before I blow your brain all over that wall."

"Rico, you'd shoot me in grandma's house at her damn table?" I asked.

Rico, with rage in his eyes, cocked his gun to let me know he was not playing any games and was ready to risk it all. Dave pulled his gun out from behind him. "Come on, Rico, don't make me go back to being this person. I'm sorry about you going to jail. I tried everything I could to keep that from happening. But when that lawyer showed those pictures of that 16-year-old girl sucking your dick and you too having that drug exchange, my hands were tied. He had won the jury over." I tried to tell Rico.

"Man, fuck, I wasn't even mad about that to you. Let them send me to the same jail that that girl's dad was in. Do you know what they did to me in there? They jumped me. The girl's dad even set it up for an inmate with HIV to rape me in the showers. Do you know how fucked my life is now? Do you know how people look at me on the streets? Do you know how it feels for your kids mothers to look at you differently. Or question you being around your own kids alone Do you," Rico yelled and waved his gun with tears in his eyes.

"Man, I'm sorry when your mom told us what happened, and that you were in the hospital every other week. I felt terrible. I didn't want none of that to happen to you. But this, we don't have to do this. We can put the guns down, man. You know me and I know you."

In the heat of the moment, and me and Rico talking, I never noticed that Amber was standing in the doorway that Rico had left open. She was standing with a gun pointing at the back of Rico's head, and he didn't even know it. When I finally saw her, she put her fingers to her lips to let me know not to say anything about her presence.

"Dave, I don't give a fuck what's done is done. With nothing else in me to say to convince Rico that this could go a totally different way, I pulled the bag of money from under the table. Then the gun went off, POW! Now give me the damn money before Auntie Dorothea will plan your funeral." Rico said letting off a warning shot into the ceiling. Before I could say anything and Rico pointed his gun at me. POW! the sound of the gun went off.

Amber

I STOOD there with my gun smoking and tears rolling down my face. This was not the person I wanted to be. I watched the blood pour from Dave's body onto the wood floors.

Rico turned around to see where the shot had come from. "Do you love me now?" I asked him. Rico picked up the bag of money and headed back towards the door. As he crossed my path, I grabbed his arm and cried out, "Rico." He looked at my hand and snatched it away.

Inside, I felt like I was the person who was lying on the floor bleeding. I had just done the unthinkable for this man. My head was racing and spinning, trying to understand how. How the hell did I get to this fucking point? The room seemed like it was closing in on me.

I rushed out of the house behind Rico, and like a madwoman, I stood behind his car in broad daylight with my gun out. I screamed, "Rico." I could see him looking at me in the rear-view mirror. I pointed the gun at Rico and said, "Rico, don't make me."

Rico got out of the car and stood in front of me, looking me dead in the eye. "You bad? Pull the shit then. I already know

I'm dying," he said to me. My hand was shaking. Rico snatched the gun and pushed me towards the house; "get your dumb ass in the house." As I walked inside, Rico looked around to see if anyone was watching us.

I came into the house, sat on the couch, still shook, and put my head into my hands. Rico came in and slammed the door. "You better be glad this the hood. People around here hear gunshots and still mind their business. That's probably why Dave wanted to meet here." Rico said, as he laughed a little.

I jumped off the couch and got in Rico's face. "What the fuck is wrong with you? You're laughing like YOUR COUSIN isn't in there laying on the floor dead." I barked. "That's not on me, that's your body. I was just trying to get my money, and now I got it," Rico said back to me. I looked at Rico and cried. "So that's it. No explanation, no nothing? You don't even care that I love you," I asked him. I need to know why. Maybe if he explained, I could walk away, and the hurt would go away.

"Tell you what, Amber?" Explain what?" Rico asked, like I was annoying him. "The truth! The fucking truth Rico." I screamed out. Rico paced. "Amber, the truth about what?" he said. "Rico, about everything," I said to him, looking at him, confused why he was playing stupid. "Rico, do you have H.I.V?" I tried to ask him in my calmest voice.

Rico looked at me again, now making eye contact. "Yes," he said. My chest felt like it had been caved in. I slapped Rico with all the might I had in me. The impact caused him to drop the gun he was holding, and it slid on the floor towards me.

Rico turned back towards me, holding the side of his face. "Okay, I deserved that," he said. "You deserved that? Nah, that's not even half of what you deserve, Rico. You had sex with me knowing you were infected and didn't say a word in the six months we been together." I screamed—Rico smirked. I couldn't understand what he possibly thought was even close to being funny.

"It's kinda hard to tell a person you're infected when they got your dick in their mouth on the first night straight after y'all walk out the club." He said to me, I reached down and grabbed the gun off the floor, and once again pointed it at Rico. "You think this a damn joke? This is my life," I said to him, no longer crying but shaking with rage. "You put my damn life in danger, and it's not just your fault. It's mine for being stupidly in love with you. I even put Dave's life at risk," I said emotionally"

Rico looked at Dave. You ain't just risk that nigga life you took it, and either way, fuck that nigga." I cocked my gun. Rico reached behind him for his gun, and the look on his face let me know he didn't have it on him. He was in such a rush that he dropped it in the bag with the money.

"So you're a walking death sentence and a pedophile?" I boldly asked him with the gun to back me up. That must have hit a nerve because Rico screamed out, "I didn't rape her. That little girl told me she was 19. I would have never sold her the drugs or let her give me head in exchange if I knew she was only 16. I'm a dad. I would kill the nigga that did that to one of my daughters." Rico pleaded for once, sounding like he gave a fuck about something.

I just looked at him. "How was I supposed to know? She was in the club getting high with some of my other normal clients." All this was so much to take in. "So you sat in jail for all these years thinking about how you were going to get back at Dave for him, not getting you off for something, YOU DID!" I said to him,

"I sat in jail and suffered, bitch. Don't act like you know my damn story. These fifty stacks are nothing compared to what I went through in there. I was alone. The only person I had was my mother, and she was out here. Dave wouldn't even bring her to come see me. Then she got sick, and he didn't even check on her. I was trying to be the head of the house from jail while going through my own shit in there. And Dave knows and didn't even hold me down like a family was supposed to do. My mom could've died if I didn't come home." Dave said to me.

I felt for Rico. I never knew about all of this. But I have to know, "how were you able to come home early, anyway?" Rico took a seat and took a deep breath. "I witnessed a murder before I went to jail, and when they came and talked to me about it, they offered me a deal. If I testified against my friend, they could cut my time and send me home on paper. Between getting jumped, getting raped, finding out I had H.I.V, and my mom being sick, I took the deal.

But now that deal caught up with me. Chase as sent people to my house. Threaten people I love and I have to do what's best for mine. I've pull together every dime I had stashed away before I went in, and its not enough. This fifty stack is, so he doesn't kill everyone I care about; my mom, my kids... I had to do what I had to do. I thought Dave's ass would pay up. I'd get the money and could disappear. Never having to explain all of this to you or anyone else."

Before I could say a word, Rico got a call. He pulled that same flip phone out of his pocket. "Shit." He said before answering.

Hello...

Yes, I got the money...

We can meet tonight...

Alright, nine is fine...

Rico hung up. "Yo, this Oprah shit is over. I got to go," Rico said as he got up. "So you're just going to leave? What about him?" I said, pointing at Dave on the floor. "See, he's your problem, not mine, that's your bullet in him. It's my job to go save my babies, and that's what I am about to do." He said and turned away. I grabbed Rico and pulled the paperwork from the clinic saying I was pregnant from my back pocket. "What about the life of the baby you put in me?" Rico pulled away from me. "Bitch, you can't blame that on me. You were fucking me and that nigga. He could be the father." He said to me,

I shook again. "Rico, it's your baby, I'm sure of it. I made love to you, not Dave." I cried out to him. He laughed at me. "I wouldn't dare cailm that baby. Bitch, you're an unloyal ass hoe. That bastard baby could belong to anyone. Even if you have it, its life is damned living with the disease that you probably now have too."

Before I knew it, my gun went off again. I snapped. When I realized what I had done, Rico was lying in front of me with a hole in his chest. I panicked and paced the floor. But the sound of a phone ringing interrupted that.

I checked Rico's pockets, but it wasn't his. Then I looked over at Dave. I walked across the room and patted his pockets in search of the phone. But I was looking at the hole I had put in Dave's stomach.

Before I could pull the phone out of Dave's pocket, his head turned towards me. His eyes opened. He seemed as if he was gasping for air and struggling to keep his eyes open. "Bitch," he muttered. I jumped back with the phone in my hand. I hit the wall behind me and slid down to the floor in a sitting position. I looked at Dave.

Then his phone rang again. I looked down at Jayden. I cleared my voice and answered the phone.

"Hello"

"Hello?" Jayden said back to me like he was confused or trying to figure out the voice.

"Hey Joc, what's up? Dave is sleeping." I said to him,

"Amber? Um, okay... Well, have that nigga hit my line when he gets up."

I hung up. "Fuck, fuck, fuck" I screamed and stomped. What the fuck was I about to do. I started pacing back and forth. I looked at the man I loved and then the man that treated me the best, laying in blood before me.

"I got to get the hell out of here," I said. I put Dave's phone back in his pocket. Then I grabbed his gun. As I looked at him for the last time, tears poured down my face. "Dave, I'm sorry" I walked over to Rico, wiped my gun off, and planted it next to him. Before I walked off, I kicked him. "I loved you."

I got to the door and peeked out. It seemed all clear, so I hurried. I grabbed the bag of money out of Rico's car and got into mine. I pulled off. I drove, and I cried. I lit a cigarette and cried more. I thought to myself, I just have to start over.

As I drove, my phone rang. It was Dave's mom. I wasn't sure what she was calling me for. I knew she hadn't figured out that quickly what happened. I shook. I pulled over and lit another cigarette. She called me again. I didn't answer. I screamed out into the empty car, "Leave me alone. Your son is dead. I killed him and Rico. But I still have one more life to take."

Chapter 23
Jayden

IT WAS SO HARD SITTING in that car and trying to act like I did not know what was going on or I didn't play a role in it. None of this shit was supposed to work out this way. I knew that bitch Amber wasn't the one for Dave, and when Brandy told me she was fucking on Rico, I knew for sure. The night he met her, I told his ass he was too sweet, and she would play him. But he still had to have her ass and fucked with her and now look. He was stuck in this dumb ass entanglement because of her. But then again, we all were in this entanglement because of Rico and the decisions we all made. From me all the way down to Chase.

"Jayden, what is going on?" Tracey asked me when I came back into the house. "Nothing," I answered as I walked past her. "Jayden, stop lying to me. I am your woman. Dave doesn't come over here." She said to me, I stopped and looked at her for a moment. Although she was right that Dave didn't come to my house ever, I wasn't telling her my business. There were things I kept her out of for her safety and peace of mind.

"We both know I don't share nothing with you unless it about our children. Not to mention didn't you just storm out my office yesterday." I said to her. Tracey walked up to me and wrapped her arms around me. "Bae, lets leave?" she said. "You can go on a vacation with the kids if you but I got stuff to do." I told her. "I am not talking about a vacation, Jayden. I mean, like let's move. Let's pack up our stuff and our child and get the hell out of here. With everything that's going on with Chase, I see you getting pulled in more and more, and I want nothing to happen to you. Me and your sons need you. So lets pack up and go. We have employees to run the businesses. We can leave all this shit behind and start fresh and new." She said to me with this look in her eyes.

"Not right now," I told her. Tracey let go of me and I could tell she felt defeated. I grabbed her hand. "Listen, I'm not saying we can't make the move. But what I am saying is that let's plan it out and do it the right way." I told her. Tracey looked me up and down and took her arm back from me, and walked off.

I went to the den and sat down, and thought about what Tracey said. Leaving might be my only way to truly get out. But I didn't want to just walk away from Chase and Dave. I didn't want to just walk away from Brandy; I liked what she and I were building. And she already felt like she had no one. I didn't want her to think I got her to open up just to fuck her over.

I dozed off for a few and when I woke up in a silent house. I got up and looked around and Tracey was gone nowhere to be found. I went back to the den to call her, and I noticed I had a missed call from Dave. I checked my voicemail, and he was telling me he was meeting up with Rico at their grandma's house. "What the fuck is this nigga thinking?" I said to myself. Pushing Tracey to the back of my head and calling Dave because why would this nigga meet with Rico on his own. I would have come with him.

I called and was surprised when Amber answered. "Hello," she answered

"Hello?" I said back to her like I was confused.

"Hey Joc, what's up? Dave is sleeping." She told me. But I didn't believe it; there was no way that Dave had hit me an hour ago, and he was already at home sleeping. and that he even was still letting this bitch Amber be around.

"Amber? Um, okay... Well, have that nigga hit my line when he gets up." I told her.

I hung up and figured Dave would get back to me, and for now. I would see what the hell was going on with Tracey. I called her phone. "Hello?" she answered. "Where are you?" I asked. "I had to leave. Jayden, I don't trust you and something is telling me you are in some shit and you're going to get us caught up in the bullshit." She said, "Tracey, what the hell are you talking about." I said. "Jayden I am not stupid you're moving different and I'm not with it." she said, "man where the hell are you with my son." I yelled. "We are fine. When you get your shit together, then call me." she said, hanging up.

This bitch had me fucked up. She could leave, but my sons was a no-go, and she knew that. I went to my find my iPhone location and to my surprise her dumb ass hadn't turned off her location and I could see right where she was with no issue.

I grabbed my keys and headed out the door. It took me an hour to get to the hotel she was staying at outside the city. I parked and ran into the front desk. "Hello," I said, smiling at the young white girl that was at the front desk. "Hey," she said in a tone that let me know she was into me. "Can you tell me what room Tracy Harris is in?" I asked her as I slid a $100 bill across the desk. She looked at the money and then backed up for sure. "For you I sure can." she said, licking her lips and not taking the money. In a few moments, she looked back at me and said, "room 415" I smiled and thanked her. And headed back to my car. I grabbed my gun from my glovebox and place it under my shirt.

Tracey was bringing her ass home willingly or by force. It was going to be completely up to her with that road she went down. I took the stairs to the fourth floor. And walked until I found the room. I took my gun out from under my shirt and prepared to knock on the door. When my phone rang. I pulled it out, and it was Ms. Dorothie. I answered quickly. "Hey ma what's going on?" I said to her, "You need to get to the hospital asap. They found Dave and Rico shot in my momma's old house," she said.

I felt life leave my body when she said those words. I looked at the door and then at my gun. All this had gone too far. Dave and Rico were shot. I was about to pull a damn gun on Tracey. This was going way too damn far. "I'm on my way," I said to her as I hung up, tucked my gun back in my pants and ran off from the door.

JAYDEN

"MS. DOROTHIE, we have your son out of surgery," the nurse came out and informed Dave's mom. "Thank God," she said with a sigh of relief. The nurse looked at her and said: "he is stable at least, but during the surgery, he slipped into a coma." The nurse's words broke her down. Like it wasn't bad enough that she found her son and nephew bleeding out in her deceased mother's home, but now her son is lying in a hospital bed in a coma, and she doesn't know why or who did it to him. But I had a good idea that it had something to do with that bitch Amber that was currently nowhere to be found.

I held Ms. Dorothie in my arms. "Jayden, who would do this to my baby?" The question broke my heart. Dave, Rico, and I had grown up as not just best friends, but brothers from diapers. When my mom lost her battle with sickle cell, Ms. Dorothea said no son of her best friend was going into the system and took me in. She gave me everything that Dave had. So today was my turn to be here for her. I just wish I could take her pain away.

As I held her and told her everything was going to be okay, the elevator door opened. I was honestly expected to see Amber step out. Maybe then my head could convince my gut was wrong. And she was innocent. But who stepped out, an older lady that looked like she was fighting for that last bit of life she had. "Hi my name is Clara Piers. I got a call that my son Rico, well, Remario Piers, was here," she said, as she looked at the nurse at the front desk. I watched as the nurse told her to hold and then grabbed a doctor.

The doctor came over and spoke to her, and you could tell he was delivering bad news. The scream Ms. Clara let out when the doctor said, "Ma'am, I am sorry we did all we could do but we pronounced your son dead 20 mintues ago." made the whole room jump and look. When Ms. Dorothie turned around and laid eyes on her sister as she ran to console her.

"Clara, I'm sorry. Clara, I'm so sorry," she said as she held her tightly. Ms. Clara screamed into her sister's chest, "not my son! Not my baby!" The way Ms. Dorotheie was loving on her sister and showing her support. You would have never known that these two ladies hadn't talked in years.

As if this day wasn't bad enough for these two ladies, out of the corner of my eye, I see a cop walking towards them. "This fucker," I said as I walked towards him to stop him. "Excuse me," he said as I stared him down. "Nah, not right now, my guy," I told him. "Are those the mothers of David Lott and Remario Piers?" he asked. "Yes it is, but right now ain't the time," I answered him. "Well, the sooner we get questioning out of the way, the quicker we can find their killer." the police officer said. "Yo, are you stupid? These ladies are hurting right now, and you think I'm letting you question them right now. You cops don't care about people or have any respect for what they are going through."

I said to him, "Sir, Mr...." I interrupted him, "Smith... Mr. Smith." "Okay, Mr. Smith, well, your Martin Luther King speech is nice, but not needed. I'm just trying to do my job." He said. "And I'm doing mine and that's protecting them from people like you!" I told him. "Are you even family?" He asked. "I'm the closest thing to it." I answered. "Those are my best friends that were found today. One is still fighting for his life and the other just lost his.. their moms are sisters and since they can't be here for their mothers, I am." I said with a mean mug. The cop tried to go around me, and I blocked him. He nodded his head. "You know what? Here's my card. When they are ready to talk, have them call me." he said as he handed me his card before walking off.

"Ass hole," I mumbled as he walked away from.

I walked over to the ladies, and I tapped Ms. Dorothie on the back. "Mom, I'm in the room with Dave, "I told her. Clara lifted her. "Dave's here too," she asked" Ms. Dorothie looked down. "Yes, I found him and Rico both at momma's house shot," she said sadly. "So my son dies and your life? This is just like before; everything goes well for Dorothie while I sit by the side and suffer." Clara retorted. I looked at her, confused. "Clara, this is not about you and me. I called the police at the same time for both boys. One didn't get better care than the other," she said to her. "Then why didn't you call me? And why did my son die while yours is still alive?" Clara asked.

"This is why this is right here. Because no matter what I do, I will always be your enemy instead of your little sister. I know you're hurting and I am so sorry my nephew is gone. But I have a son laying in a coma and a daughter-in-law that I am beyond worried about because no one can find her. When you can see, it's about these young people and finding out who did this to them. Then we can bond together as sisters and be there for each other." Ms. Dorothea said as she walked away.

I stood there with my face twisted, trying to understand what was really going on before me. As Ms. Dorothie walked off, Ms. Clara screamed out. "Fuck you, Dorothie!" It was kind of funny to see an old lady cuss as hard as she did. But it was painful. When we were kids, Ms. Dorothie and my mom raised Rico and Dave not to put anything before family. And right now, these two needed family more than ever, and they couldn't seem to get it together.

Ms. Dorothie turned around. "Clara, what is wrong with you? Whatever our differences are doesn't matter right now. You are my sister. That is your son and my nephew that they just pronounced dead. In the room down the hall lies my son and your nephew that they have in a coma. We need each other. I loved Rico and you..."

Ms. Clara cut Ms. Dorthea off in the middle of her speech. "Don't you dare stand here and lie. Don't say you love or care about my son. We all know that you couldn't stand Rico or the air he breathed, all because he was your stepson, not just your nephew."

I swear this was some shit that you would see on tv. My jaw hit the floor. I wasn't sure if I was supposed to stay around for more tea, go to the room with Dave, or break up this heated conversation.

Ms. Dorothie's mouth tightened as she said, "so that is what you still stuck on. Well, since we are bringing up old news, let me make some things clear. I never hated him, you did! For the first 10 years of that boy's life, you were gone. And yes big sis, I understand you were hurting because my husband raped you. But had your ass not always been drunk and high, you could've kept a job and kept your under the influence ass off my couch where Darren could take advantage of you." she said as she stepped closer to her sister.

"Dorothie, you're still a damn fool. Over 20 years later and you're still sticking up for the fucked up things Darren did. I hope his money is worth it because you're going to burn in hell. But just so I can make myself clear; if you're going to tell my sad story, at least tell it right. I didn't walk out on my son. I left him with his father while I got myself together. And when his father died, I came and got him." Ms. Clara said back while looking Ms. Dorothie straight in the eyes.

"No, you came back for a check. You found out Darren died and came back with your hand out. You didn't care about your son or how he had been for the last ten years. You wanted to know what money Rico would get out of it since he was Darren's son. When I refused to give you any of Rico's inheritance, you took him away from the home and family he knew and disappeared.

I raised him for ten years. I loved him like he was my own. No, I never told him or Dave that they were brothers because that was not my job, that was for their father to handle. But I made sure these boys were loved, well taken care of, and never felt like one was better than the other. And when you took Rico from us, I searched high and low for you all.

I was willing to let you move into my home so that I could know that Rico was safe. When Darren died, the boys were all I had because my sister had already left me because of something out of my control. So don't you dare tell me I don't care or that I didn't love Rico." Ms. Dorothie said, fighting back the tears.

"You raised MY SON for ten years because you felt bad, not because you had to. Had you been a better wife and taken care of home and your husband, your husband would have never touched me." Ms. Clara said, stepping closer to Ms. Dorothie.

"Clara, you're hurt. Go home. I got to go check on my son. When you come to your senses, call me. So we can bury Rico the right way and make sure those grandbabies are good." Ms. Dorothie said as she turned to walk away again.

I followed Ms. Dorothie down the hall to Dave's room. I

could feel Ms. Clara burning a hole in the back of our heads until we were out of her sight. When we got to the door, Ms. Dorothie said, "Any update on Amber?" I answered her quickly. "No, ma'am." "I need you to do some research; my guts keep telling me something isn't right. I'm hoping she isn't somewhere dead, hurt, or in danger," she said to me. "Yes, ma'am, I will get right on it," I told her as I pulled my phone out. "Thank you, baby. Lord knows I am in no mood to tell anyone else about the wellbeing of their child." I just shook my head.

I walked down the hall and dialed a number. "Jayden, one more thing," she said. I turned around. "Yes ma'am," I answered. "Find out who put the bullets in MY SONS because I want them to know and feel my wrath as a mother."

As I walked away, I mumbled to myself. "If she's lucky, then she's dead already because my gut says Amber did this." I took out my phone and dialed a number.

"Hey Daddy."

"Not right now, Brandy. Where the fuck is your sister?"

To Be continued....

Author Breanna J ORDER FORM

www.authorbreannaj.com

INMATES ONLY receive novels for $10.00 per book PLUS shipping fee PER BOOK.

(Mail Order MUST come from inmate directly to receive discount)

Book Title	Price	Check to order
In the name of love	$10.99	
In the name of Love 2	$12.99	
The Cost of Love	$15.00	
No More secrets	$12.99	
Feeling	$15.00	
Pleasurable Desire	$18.00	
The Entanglement	$13.00	

Please add **$5.00** for shipping and handling fees for up to **(2) BOOKS PER ORDER**. (INMATES INCLUDED) PUBLICATIONS ADDRESS:

P.O. BOX 24921

Rochester NY 14624

CUSTOMER'S NAME: _____

ADDRESS: _____

CITY/STATE: _____

CONTACT/EMAIL: _____

Please Allow 8-10 Business Days Before Shipping NOTE: Due to COVID-19 Some Orders May Take Up To 3 Weeks Before They Ship We are NOT responsible for Prison Orders rejected NO RETURNS and NO REFUNDS * NO PERSONAL CHECKS ACCEPTED * STAMPS NO LONGER ACCEPTED

Made in the USA
Columbia, SC
01 March 2022